EMMETT
& GENTRY

an Emmett Love Western - Volume 3
John Locke

TELEMACHUS PRESS

This book is a work of fiction. Names, characters, places and incidents are either the product of the author's imagination or are used fictitiously. Any resemblance to actual persons, living or dead, or to actual events or locales is entirely coincidental.

EMMETT & GENTRY

The publisher does not have any control over and does not assume any responsibility for author or third-party websites or their content.

Cover Designed by: Telemachus Press, LLC

Cover Art :
Copyright © shutterstock 75950503/Alan Poulson Photography
Copyright © shutterstock 110213159/Alan Poulson Photography
Copyright © shutterstock 21929821/bubaone

Published by: Telemachus Press, LLC
http://www.telemachuspress.com

Visit the author website:
http://www.donovancreed.com

ISBN: 978-1-937698-34-8 (Paperback)
ISBN: 978-1-937387-80-8 (eBook)

Printed in the United States of America

10 9 8 7 6 5 4 3 2 1

EMMETT
& GENTRY

PROLOGUE

Two Years Earlier...

I

FOURTEEN-YEAR-OLD Faith Coulter moved through the thick fog of an east Texas dawn with tear-stained cheeks. Two hours ago she walked out the front door of her parents' farmhouse like she always did at five a.m. to milk the cows, only this time she walked right past the barn, climbed over the fence, crossed the crick, and never looked back. Just put one foot in front of the other and soldiered on. Didn't start bawling till she got within hollering distance of the steep bluffs of the Red River, where she intended to take her life.

Why was she throwing her life away?

Loose bowels.

She had loose bowels four months ago, what her father referred to as "the drizzlin' shits." That night Faith had found herself in dire straits shortly after supper. By midnight, fearing her lower gut might explode, she ran to the outhouse and spent the next twenty minutes sitting on the wooden toilet bench making more noise than most would consider polite. Under such miserable circumstances, she was happy to be alone.

Till she heard a man's voice.

"Ever been to Kansas?" he said, from the other side of the door.

Faith's body tensed and she gasped loudly. She'd been startled, but wasn't frightened because the voice outside was so friendly and conversational she instinctively knew there was nothing to fear. Of course, she was embarrassed about her condition and the sounds she'd made. Had he heard her? Yes, of course he had. That's how he knew she was in the outhouse in the first place.

But should she answer? Or pretend she hadn't heard him? If she remained silent, he'd probably move along. She decided not to answer.

But he spoke again.

"Sounds like you're feelin' poorly. No need to be ashamed, we all get sick now and again. Take your time. When you finish up, I'll escort you back to your door safely."

"I'll be fine," Faith said.

"Normally, I'd agree," the man said. "But I've been trackin' a scoundrel more than 400 miles, and know him to be in these parts. You'll want to trust me when I say he's not a moral man."

Faith normally wiped herself with summer leaves from the pile on the outhouse floor. But on this occasion she knew her bottom was particularly messy, and it was dark in the outhouse, which meant using leaves would soil her fingers and require a journey to the crick. That's what she'd expected to do, use the leaves, then wash her hands in the crick. But it wouldn't be right to make the man wait. Her alternative was to use her father's old sock that hung from the nail on the side wall. She could use that, and wash it in the morning. Perhaps her father wouldn't be upset, knowing how sick her stomach had been.

She reached for the sock and wiped her bottom carefully, then hung the soiled sock back on the nail.

"I don't know your voice," Faith said. "Who are you?"

"Emmett Love. Sheriff, Dodge City, Kansas."

Faith got her nightclothes situated, sniffed her fingers to make sure they were clean, then said, "I'm coming out now, sheriff."

When she opened the door he stood to the side to let her pass. As she did, he grabbed her from behind and said, "Make a sound and I'll kill you. Then I'll kill your parents."

II

FAITH WAS SO startled she began screaming before his words registered. But to her surprise, the only sound that came from her throat was a hiss. She felt his bicep between her neck and right shoulder, his arm across her chest, and his hand gripping her left armpit. She felt his hip pivot and dig into her back, and suddenly found herself tilted backward and moving, her heels dragging the dirt as he pulled her behind the outhouse. Moments later he kicked her legs out from under her, and she hit the ground hard. He lay on top of her, placed his left hand over her mouth, lifted her nightshirt and despoiled her right there in the dirt. When he was done, he told her to wait five minutes before going back in the house.

"You can tell your parents if you want to," he said. "But if I hear about it, I'll kill them."

He pulled his pants back up, started to leave. Then turned back, got down on one knee and said, "I'm sparin' you because you got grit. You never cried out once, though I know it was your first time." He paused a minute before adding, "I'm sorry this happened. I mean, that it happened to you instead of someone else. But you're gonna be alright."

But Faith wasn't alright.

He'd got her pregnant.

That much became clear within two months. Her response was to double her work load on the farm, hoping her increased labor would kill the baby. But it didn't, and now she was starting to show. Soon her ma would know, and then her dad, and Faith could deal with them knowing, but it wouldn't stop there. Her father would eventually strap on a gun and ride off to find Sheriff Love, and get himself killed in the process. And she'd still have a bastard child to raise, one whose presence would remind her every day that her father had lost his life because of her loose bowels.

Faith could let all that happen, or simply take her life.

She stopped crying and worked her way through the bull pines till she came to the edge of the highest cliff. From there, she looked down at the river. It was a sixty foot drop and she couldn't swim. She figured to die from the fall, but took comfort knowing if she didn't, at least she'd drown. She closed her eyes and wondered what drowning would feel like. Deciding she had nothing to compare it to, she bent her legs and prepared to jump.

A voice behind her said, "*Don't!*"

Faith gasped, opened her eyes, turned her head. Saw a young woman sitting on a large rock, twenty feet away.

"It's okay, Faith," the woman said. "I'm here."

Faith was stunned to hear her name coming from the woman's lips.

"Who *are* you?" she said.

"I'm Rose. I know everything about you, and I'm here to help."

Faith turned her head back toward the river.

"Don't do it," Rose said.

v

"I-I have to."

"No."

"You don't understand," Faith said.

"I understand everything. But it's okay. I have a plan."

Faith bit her lip.

"*I have a plan*," Rose repeated.

Faith paused a moment, then took a step back.

"What do you know about me?" she said.

III

"THE MAN WHO got you pregnant," Rose said.

"Emmett Love. Sheriff of Dodge City, Kansas."

"It wasn't Sheriff Love."

"It was! He told me his name. That's why I trusted him."

"Come," Rose said. "Sit." She patted the empty space on the rock beside her. Faith moved closer, but remained standing. Rose said, "Emmett Love is a decent man. He's my friend, captured four months ago by the Union Army at Fort Bend, Kansas."

"Then who attacked me and left me with child?"

"Bose Rennick."

Faith gasped. "The *outlaw*?"

Rose nodded.

"How do you know all this?" Faith asked.

"You'll think me crazy if I say."

Faith searched Rose's eyes, and said, "Please. Tell me anyway."

Rose said, "I've waited more than two hundred years for this to happen."

CHAPTER 1

Emmett Love.
Present Day...

THE HARDEST PART about walkin' to Dodge City in the middle of the night is keepin' Rudy from followin' me. I mean, this is one hell of a lonely bear.

I don't know how long he's been out here all alone, and it breaks my heart to leave him. But I can't take him with me, since I don't know what to expect in Dodge. So after playin' a few games of tag, I try to force him back to the woods.

But he keeps followin' me.

I push him harder, but he's determined to come. I yell at him and push him some more, and he finally sits on the

1

ground and pouts like a child. When I turn to leave he starts cryin'. I hate walkin' away from him, but I do, and he makes it worse by bawlin' somethin' pitiful. After a half mile I can still hear him in the background, and each cry is more sorrowful than the one before, and each tugs at my heart. But I need to find Gentry, and hope Rudy'll stay in the general area till I come back to get him. And I can't do that till I know why Gentry or someone else brought him here in the first place.

I walk on.

As I do, I think about the life Gentry and I had in Dodge City twenty-eight months ago when we owned the *Lucky Spur*. I ran the saloon and card emporium, and she ran the five whores upstairs. We'd just hired a Chinese cook and handyman named Wing Ding, and I'd recently become sheriff of Dodge, when I shot and killed Sam Hartman, one of the most notorious outlaws who ever lived. Sam traveled with a stone-cold killer named Bose Rennick, who's tried to kill me numerous times for various reasons. I'm sure I ain't seen the last of Bose, since he and Sam were rumored to have kinfolk all over Texas, Oklahoma, and Kansas.

About the time I killed Sam Harman, my witchy friend, Rose, had a vision of a slaughter she believed would take place in Lawrence, Kansas. So she and Gentry headed there by wagon to warn the town. I left a day later on horseback, plannin' to catch up to 'em on the trail. In Rose's vision a former schoolteacher named William Clarke sacked the town and killed hundreds of men and boys. I did leave Dodge the next day, but was shot by some Union soldiers who mistook me for a horse thief. Next thing I know me and fifty rebel prisoners were forced to build a Union railroad. In a crazy twist of fate, yesterday, after twenty-eight months' imprisonment, I was set free by the same man who killed all them people in Rose's vision! Clarke told me I'd been held prisoner by the Union Army for twenty-eight months!

No matter. I'm free, and walkin' to Dodge 'cause it's the likeliest place my Gentry would go to wait for me. In a perfect world she'd be servin' customers at the *Spur*, and workin' the girls upstairs, and makin' lots of money. She'd be healthy, and happy to see me.

But of course, it ain't a perfect world.

The north and south are at war, and Kansas is right smack in the middle of it. Rudy the bear was Gentry's pet, and lived in our saloon. The fact that Rudy is now livin' in the woods don't make me feel the least bit good about what might've happened to Gentry and the *Spur*.

I got a lot to worry about.

I need to find Gentry, or at least find out what's happened to her. I need to know what's become of my best friends, Shrug and Rose. Shrug's a capable scout, and Rose is quite possibly a witch. Between the two of 'em, they should've been able to find me these past twenty-eight months, had they been lookin'.

Had they been alive.

I've got other worries.

I'm wearin' Union pants, which means northern soldiers might take me for a deserter, while southern soldiers might take me for a yankee. I could get shot either way.

And I'm wearin' leg irons.

The irons had been attached to each other with a three-foot length of chain I managed to chop in two with an axe after bein' set free yesterday. I bound each length of chain to my legs with twine I found in a railroad car.

Two years and four months. That's how long I've been in leg irons. They've chafed my ankles unmercifully, and I'm ready to be shed of 'em. As hard as the chain was to cleave, I s'pect I won't be able to get the leg irons off without the help of Dodge City's blacksmith, Tom Collins.

If Gentry's at the *Spur*, I'll spend the day in her arms and nothin' else'll matter. But I'm half expectin' to learn she's in Springfield, Missouri, with Rose and Hannah, the little orphan girl Rose is raisin'. If that's the case, my first stop'll be the *Spur*, to see what's become of the place. If Gentry's not runnin' it, someone else will be, and I'll give 'em a proper thank you, and put on a pair of my old pants and a clean shirt. I'll pull some cash from the register, find Tom and get him to remove my leg irons. Then I'll buy a gun. If there's enough money I'll buy a horse. If not, and Gentry's for sure in Springfield, I'll gladly walk the entire way, though it be 400 miles.

It's gettin' close to daybreak when I see the hill where I saved Shrug a couple years ago after he got shot by three rowdies. Within minutes I'm crossin' the field where Gentry and I started a picnic that same day. When I get to the tree where we tied the horses, I close my eyes and try to remember it.

April.

Not a cloud in the sky.

Gentry had worn a burgundy coat with lots of buttons, and a matchin' hat. The breeze was slight, unusual for that time of year. I open my eyes and look to the west, where I know the Arkansas River comes to within a hundred yards of this spot. But it's hidden by trees, and still too dark to see much detail at that distance.

I turn and look at the ground where Gentry spread the picnic blanket that day. I remember she sat on it with her back perfectly straight, like she was posin' for a portrait. I walk to the spot where she sat, and drop to one knee. I know it's impractical, but can't stop myself from placin' my palm on the ground.

I sigh deeply. My heart aches. I stay there a few minutes more, tryin' to capture that moment from long ago, but it don't take. I'm itchin' to find my woman, and these sentimental feelin's ain't gonna put me in her arms any sooner.

Less than an hour later I'm standin' on the low rise that overlooks the town. It's daybreak, and I'm surprised there ain't much activity goin' on. Problem with Dodge, it's on the old trapper trail, but twelve miles south of the east-west trail settlers began taking to Colorado a few years ago. Settlers that might be lookin' for a couple evenin's of fun will think twice before goin' twenty-four miles outta their way.

Despite the fact there ain't much activity, my pulse is racin'. I could be minutes away from Gentry. I trudge steadily toward town, though the closer I get, the more obvious it becomes.

Dodge City is practically a ghost town.

CHAPTER 2

I PICK UP my pace and enter the north side of town, lookin' for any signs of life. I see a couple of fellers on the far end of the main street, up where Jim Bigsby has his livery stable.

Or had it.

I head straight to the *Spur*, and see it's boarded up and deserted. I kick the door several times, in case anyone's inside, but no one comes. I go around the back and climb the stairs to the landin' where the whores used to smoke their hand-rolled cigarettes. Once there, I try the bedroom doors and find 'em locked, but all the windows are broken from rocks kids have thrown, so I kick most of the glass out of one of 'em, and carefully step inside.

I'm in the room where Rose had her vision of William Clarke attackin' the city of Lawrence.

I walk through the small room and out the front door, and head left on the hallway that overlooks the main room of the saloon. I stop a minute and call Gentry's name. I'm at the place she shot a blast of rock salt from her shotgun the night she got mad at me for dancin' with Rudy the bear. I turn to the right and smile, seein' that the hole she shot in the wall is still there. I look down and see what's left of the piano I shot up that same night, though the sign I put on it is gone. Our whore, Constance, lettered the sign. It said, *Music will get you shot!*

I smile at that, too, and all the other memories that come floodin' back into my head. Then I walk to the bedroom where Gentry and I used to sleep. Inside, I see my name written on the walls. Not once on each wall, but hundreds of times. With two hearts in front of 'em. And after my name is a sign that means "and," and then another name, and two more hearts.

The words between the hearts say Emmett & Gentry, and there must be a thousand of 'em written on these walls, and when I look at 'em and think of all the sad hours it took to write 'em, I'm sure my eyes would've welled up with tears if a shot hadn't been fired through the front door just then.

CHAPTER 3

I LOOK OUT the back window to see if I'm bein' set up for a cross-fire, but the back yard's clear. I unlock the back bedroom door anyway, and push it open, as a means of retreat. Then I peer out the bedroom door and watch as the front door of the saloon gets kicked down. A giant man enters, one I've met before.

"Emmett?" he hollers. "Is that you?"

I check to see he's put his gun back in his holster. Then I shout, "It's me, Jim. You aim to shoot me?"

Jim Bigsby laughs. "Hell no!"

"Then why'd you shoot the door and kick it down?"

"I didn't know who might be inside. I don't abide folks stealin' from my friends."

I come out the door, walk to the end of the hallway, and head down the steps. When Jim sees what's become of my appearance, he shakes his head.

"You're a soldier? Got yourself captured?"

We shake hands, warmly.

I say, "Where's Gentry?"

He gives me a long look. Says, "Let's sit a minute."

There's only six chairs left in the saloon that once held sixty, and all are on their sides on the floor. Jim and I pick up two of 'em, place 'em on opposite sides of a table, and sit.

I repeat, "Where's Gentry?"

"You don't know?"

I frown. "If I knew, I wouldn't have asked. What's become of her?"

He removes his hat and says, "I honestly don't know. She just...disappeared one morning."

"What do you mean?"

"One night she's here, next morning she's gone. And I never heard anyone speak about her again, except to wonder what happened."

I search his face for truth until I'm satisfied that's what I'm gettin'. Then ask, "When did she leave?"

He looks up and to the left, like he's tryin' to remember. After a bit he says, "About six months, more or less." Then adds, "I wouldn't wear them pants around here if I was you. Specially with them leg irons."

"I'm not a soldier, you dang fool. I was on my way to meet Gentry in Lawrence, Kansas, and got bushwhacked by Union soldiers outside of Fort Bend. They put me in chains and forced me to work on the railroad. I did that for twenty-eight months till yesterday, when I got rescued by southern sympathizers."

"But the pants, Emmett."

"I wore mine till they were in tatters. When one of the rebs died, I took his pants. Wore 'em till I got rescued. Then stripped one of the dead guards and kept his pants. It was that, or go naked."

"I would a' gone naked."

"What's got into you, Jim?"

"Twelve thousand and counting," he says.

"What's that mean?"

"In the past two years Kansas has lost twelve thousand men and boys. And more are getting killed every day."

"I thought Kansas was neutral."

"It was, but that didn't last long. Started out north against south, but quickly turned into cousin against cousin, father against son, and brother against brother. Damned, cursed war."

"And Dodge has turned north? Or south?"

"Both. What's left of it."

"You're still here," I say.

"I figured people will always need horses. Unfortunately, the army stole my good ones. Now me and the missus and some of the widows are eating the lame horses one at a time, hoping the war will finally end and people will come back."

"Tryin' to wait it out?"

"Still got the livery and barn. And like I say, people will always need horses."

I look around at the empty saloon. "But not a place to drink?"

"Problem with saloons, it's a social..." he pauses, searching for a word. Then says, "This is the most talking I've done in months. I can't think of enough words to explain it. So I'll just say that when all the men ran off to fight, only the women and kids were left. And they don't generally drink or whore. When news came back their husbands and sons were dead, they cleared out. One business after another went under, and your whores couldn't find work, except for deserters, and they rarely felt the obligation to pay."

"What about the Chinese? What happened to them?"

"They all moved to Colorado."

"Why?"

"The country's buildin' a railroad to connect the west to the east. The Chinese are gifted at workin' for low wages."

I nod, knowin' that to be true. Then say, "Tell me what you remember about Gentry."

"That time you and her left for Lawrence, she was gone a long time." He thinks about it. "A month, maybe? No, longer than that. Six weeks, probably. Anyway, she come back, looking for you. Went door-to-door and farm to farm. Spoke to everyone in this part of Kansas, I reckon, askin' if they'd seen or heard from you."

"You spoke to her?"

"Many times."

"How'd she seem on them occasions?"

"Heartbroken."

I nod. "That would've been June, 1861?"

"Somewhere around then."

And she stayed here from then all the way till six months ago? That's what, twenty months?"

"I'm not good at ciphering dates, but that sounds about right."

"Well, did the saloon stay in business all that time?"

"Oh, hell no! She closed the *Spur* in March of sixty-two."

"What makes you so sure of the date?"

"It's the same month we buried Roy."

"Who's Roy?"

"My nephew. Gut shot at Boley Crick. Made it all the way to our yard before dyin'. Got there in the middle of the night. We didn't even know he was outside our window till we heard the town dogs fightin' over his body."

"Sorry to hear that."

He nods.

I do the cipherin' in my head before sayin', "So she stayed here about a year after closin' the place?"

He thinks on it a minute, and says, "About that."

I look around the room. "And the whores?"

"They left when she closed."

"So it was just her alone in the place?"

"Wing Ding stayed as long as he could, to protect her and the bear."

"What do you mean?"

13

"When the town started fallin' apart, everyone put their thoughts on the bear. 1862 was a harsh winter. Folks were starvin'. They wanted to kill the bear and share the meat."

"Which folks?"

"Half the town and all the Chinese. Even a few Indians."

"It was half the town against Gentry and Wing Ding?"

"Them and some sort a' grasshopper man who jumped from rooftop to rooftop chuckin' rocks to the point people were afraid to walk the streets."

I smile, despite the harshness of his words. My old scout and best friend, Shrug, is an uncommon rock thrower. I've seen him take out ten men at a time with nothin' more than a sack of rocks and the cover of darkness. If I was goin' to war in a town like Dodge, I'd take Shrug over a troop of soldiers.

"It ain't funny. He killed at least six people."

"No, it ain't funny. Why did the Indians and Chinese want Rudy?"

"Same reason, food. But the Chinese thought him bad luck and the Indians thought the opposite. To them, black bear's a sign of power. They figured to kill the bear and drink his blood, so they could own its power. Course the Indians were afraid of the grasshopper man, so they gave up quick. On the other hand, the Chinese blamed the bear for all the bad luck that hit the town."

"That's crazy."

"Maybe. But anyway, your Gentry had her hands full, with everyone tryin' to kill her bear." He points to the corner of the saloon where Rudy used to sleep. Then he said, "She kept him in that corner over there, sat in front of him in a rockin' chair all night long with a loaded shotgun in her lap, Wing Ding watchin' the upstairs, and keepin' an eye on the baby."

I'm noddin' as he speaks, but his last word catches me by surprise.

"The *what?*"

"The baby."

"What baby?"

"Why, yours and Gentry's, of course."

CHAPTER 4

"GENTRY HAD A baby?"

"You didn't know?"

"A 'course I didn't know, you chucklehead! I've been workin' on the railroad!"

"All the live-long day?"

"What?"

"The song."

"What song?"

"Forget it."

"What kind of baby is it?"

Jim looks at me like I've lost my mind. "A human baby, of course."

"*What?*"

"A human baby. What did you think?"

I take a deep breath and let it out slowly. "Did Gentry birth a girl or boy?"

"Girl."

I nod. "And you think I'm the father?"

"That's Gentry's claim, and I reckon she'd know."

I pause before speakin'. "I know you're not overly good at cipherin' dates, Jim, but think it through, and tell me the truth. I won't hold you accountable less you lie to me."

"Lie about what?"

"Do the dates work out?"

"What dates?"

"I last saw Gentry in late April, 1861. When was the baby born?"

He thinks about it and says, "three weeks before Christmas."

"Which Christmas?"

"1861."

"You're sure?"

"Positive. Gentry showed signs of motherhood soon after she came back to Dodge. She had the baby before they put up the Christmas tree."

"The what?"

"A cattle guy from England come through town just before Christmas and bought drinks for all the card players in the saloon to celebrate Christmas. He told Gentry about how back in England they always put a pine tree in the house and decorate it to celebrate the season. Well, Gentry's eyes lit up like a little kid's, and the very next morning she had Wing Ding take the buckboard up to the river to cut a pine tree. She tore her fanciest dress into ribbons and she and the whores tied the ribbons all over the tree. Never saw anything like it! She loved that tree."

"Sounds just like her."

"She said it was a present for the baby. Said every year from that day on she was gonna have a Christmas tree in her house."

"And that was 1861."

"It was."

"You're sure?"

He looks at me.

"Of *course* it was 1861, Emmett, because the whores helped her decorate the tree. And the whores were all gone by March, 1862, when she closed the durn place."

I feel my face break out in a wide grin.

The dates match! I'm a father!

"What's her name?"

"Whose name?"

"My daughter."

He scrunches his face up a minute, thinkin' about it. "If you said it, I'd know. But the plain truth is, I'm not good with knowing baby's names. Clara would know. You can ask her at dinner tonight, if you'd care to join us."

I bet there weren't ten kids born in the whole town in 1861, and Jim can't put a name to mine. I briefly wonder how many kids Mavis Manson has popped out since I've been gone. She'd birthed fourteen before turnin' thirty.

"Thanks for tellin' me all them things," I say. "Can I trouble you for two more questions?"

"Of course."

"What became of Shrug?"

"Who?"

"The rock-thrower."

"He disappeared too."

"Same time as Gentry and the baby?"

"About the same time."

"You're sure?"

"Damn sure. I'm one of the only people he didn't hit with a rock."

"How'd you escape it?"

"I give him no reason to bother me."

"We're quiet a minute. Then he says, "What's your second question?"

"Is Tom Collins still in Dodge?"

"What's left of him."

"What do you mean?"

"He give up an arm and leg in battle."

"Is he still smithin'?"

"Nope."

"Is there another blacksmith?"

"Nope. Not much work for 'em."

"I need to get these chains cut off my ankles."

"You also need some new pants."

Suddenly Jim shouts, *Jededia!* His eyes are big as plates and he's pointin' upward and behind me while jumpin' out of his chair and backin' up.

I turn and look. Then shake my head.

"Relax," I say. "It's Rudy."

CHAPTER 5

RUDY MAKES A sound like a trumpet, which I know to be his laugh. Then he ambles his big body down the stairs, walks over to his corner, yawns, and lies down. He closes his eyes. Before Jim and me have time to say much about it, Rudy's sound asleep, and snorin'.

"I'll be damned," Jim says.

I'm frownin' on the outside, but glad to see my bear again. I say, "You think my clothes are still in the closet upstairs?"

"You didn't check while you were up there?"

"You came in too quick."

"I doubt many folks would dare to steal your clothes."

"Stay put a minute," I say, as I get to my feet.

Jim gives a nervous look at the bear.

"Don't shoot him," I say. "I'll be right back."

I climb the stairs to my bedroom and check the closet. In the corner, on the floor, are two shirts and a pair of pants. I remove my clothes and work the pants over the leg irons, pull them up and find they're huge on me. It's only now I can tell how much weight I've lost over the past two years. I put on one of the shirts and find it baggy. I'm sure I look like a kid wearin' his pa's clothes. Still, these duds aren't as apt to get me killed as a soldier's uniform, less I cross paths with a gun-totin' tailor.

The shoes I'm wearin' ain't great, but they'll do for now. I'll trade 'em in for a pair of boots after I get these blamed leg irons off.

I go back downstairs, holdin' my pants up with my left hand.

Jim Bigsby laughs.

"I s'pect Gentry and the baby are in Springfield," I say. "I aim to go there, soon as I can get this hardware off my legs. Do you have a horse I can use?"

"They're lame," Emmett.

"How lame?"

"We've eaten four so far. Got two left."

"That's pretty lame," I agree.

"Clara and me are feeding horse stew to nine others every night at our place," he says. "We'd be pleased to have you join us while you're in town."

I give him a long look. "You and Clara are good people," I say.

"Well, I like to think whoever owned lame horses would do the same for us."

Anyone in town have a good horse? And a gun and holster?"

"Not around here, less you've got gold."

"My credit's no good?"

"Not for a horse."

"Why's that?"

"There ain't any extras. Would you give up your only horse if a feller needed a ride?" He adds, "Let me think on which widow might have a gun you can borrow."

"Do that," I say. Then I ask, "Does Tom still live on Third Street?"

"He does. But he don't smith anymore."

"I aim to change that," I say.

CHAPTER 6

TOM COLLINS IS in bad shape, but we're friends, and I think he'll help.

"Got any whiskey left?" he says.

"Do I look like I got whiskey?"

He laughs. "You look like you went through all your whiskey last night."

"You too," I say.

It's true. Tom's down to one arm and one leg, and the rest of him is yellow, 'cept his fingers and toes, which are swollen and black. There's a scent comin' off his body that ain't too far off the smell Gentry's pimple poultice used to give, meanin' it's strong enough to make my eyes water. Tom's hair is thin and patchy, and looks like someone pulled it out in thick chunks. He's thin as a six-day corpse, and has a beard the color and texture of Spanish moss. He's wearin' no shoes or shirt, and his chest is all yellow with black spots, and sunk in worse than his cheeks. Lucky for Tom—if there's any luck to be found—the limbs he does have are on the same side of his body, so it appears he can get around to some extent with the use of a crutch.

"Hell of a war," he says. "Glad you escaped it."

I pull up my pants leg.

He frowns. "How long you had that?"

"Long enough. That's why I'm here."

He shakes his head. "I can't help you."

"You still got your fire pit?"

He nods.

I say, "I'm strong enough to do the work, if you're healthy enough to instruct me."

"Ain't no tools in Kansas that'll cut leg irons off."

Before I can speak he says, "There is a way. But you don't want to know it."

"Anythin' short of cuttin' my feet off will work for me."

"That's easy to say now."

"Whatever this way is that you know about," I say, "would you do it to get your leg back?"

He thinks a minute. "Maybe."

"Then let's do 'er."

I help Tom to his work area, and he explains how much wood we'll need to build the fire.

"About all I've got to my name is wood," I say. "I can use the tables and chairs. If that ain't enough I can use some of the railin's."

He chuckles. "It's gonna take all the railin's, doors, and half the walls."

"How's that possible?"

"You're gonna have to build lots of fires. You'll gather wood at night, burn it durin' the day."

"What's the plan?"

He says, "Only way I know to do this is wedge as much cloth as you can between the leg iron and your ankle, all around. Then you're gonna spoon water on the cloth. Then you're gonna take that poker over there and set the tip of it into the fire till it's white hot. Then you're gonna push the tip of that poker into the leg iron till it cools. Then back over the fire till it's hot again. Then back in the same spot till it cools. You're gonna do that as long as you can stand it until you burn a hole all the way through. Then you're gonna start all over again till you make the next hole next to the first one."

He looks at the leg iron. "You'll have to make about six holes, then burn through the iron that separates the holes."

"How long will that take?"

"Depends on how much you can stand. The poker's white hot, so you'll have to protect your hands, which makes for awkward work when workin' on yourself. After a minute, the leg iron will be as hot as the poker. You'll want a bucket of water to dip onto the cloth every few minutes, to keep the flesh on your ankles from boilin'. But you've got open wounds there, so after about ten minutes it'll feel like you're gettin' branded."

"Suppose I can handle the pain. How long would it take to get the first leg iron off?"

"Two weeks."

"*What?*"

"Give or take. And you need to be careful toward the end of each hole, just before the poker goes through, because if you're pushin' too hard at that point, you can burn yourself beyond repair."

"What about the chains?"

"What about 'em?"

"If you were me, would you get rid of the chains first? Or let 'em come off with the cuffs?"

He thinks on it a minute before sayin', "If it was me, I'd take the extra time to get the chains off. It'll lighten your load and make it easier for you to get around over the next month while you burn holes in the leg irons."

"How long will it take to burn through the chains?"

"About a day or two for each."

"I'll start fetchin' wood," I say.

"You can stack it in here," he says.

I nod. "You got a gun?"

"I do not."

"You sure?"

"I'm still alive, ain't I?"

CHAPTER 7

I'M MISERABLE THINKIN' about the delay. I've also got nothin' for Rudy to eat. I borrow a rope from Tom, and a large flour sack. I use the rope to tie my pants around my waist, and figure to fill the sack with tubers from a field east of town where tubers have always been plentiful, if you know where to dig. It's six miles each way, and I'm hopin' Rudy will help me gather enough for a week of meals.

I tie the sack to my rope belt and head back to the *Spur* and try to get Rudy up.

He's tired.

"You're makin' this twice as hard on me," I say loudly.

Rudy opens one eye, then closes it, and settles back to sleep. I check his feet.

They're fine, which makes no sense.

Rudy had been terribly abused by his original owners, who taught him to dance by beatin' him and burnin' his feet on hot plates. By the time I acquired him, his feet were so bad he was nearly crippled. On the one hand I know a bear's feet can't be healed after a lifetime of abuse. On the other hand, Rudy's feet have not only been healed, they look perfect. I think on it a minute and decide my witchy friend, Rose, must a' given Gentry some sort of poultice to put on 'em.

I'm concerned but not afraid to leave Rudy at the *Spur*. There aren't many people left in Dodge to harm him, and he's been out in the wild long enough to know when danger's afoot. I'd feel better if he came with me, but don't have time to wait for him to finish his nap. I've got to walk twelve miles round trip in the burnin' heat of an August day with leg irons and chains.

When I get back, I'll start collectin' wood for the fire I'll need to build tomorrow. I walk to the front door of the *Spur*, turn, and look up at the door to the bedroom where me and Gentry used to sleep.

"I'm comin' honey," I say. "You'll just have to wait awhile longer."

Then I lift my weary feet down the street and start makin' my way toward the tuber field, six miles away.

Three hours later I'm exhausted. But my day ain't half over, so I try to focus on the stand of poplars three hundred yards in the distance, where I hope to find an abundance of tubers for Rudy. Beyond bein' tired, my problems include the diggin', the carryin', the walk back to Dodge, and the two young Indians at the top of the rise who just spotted me.

Now that they're trottin' toward me, yippin', I can say they've just become my biggest problem.

CHAPTER 8

THERE'S TWO OF 'em, ridin' the same horse. They're young, maybe fifteen. I see no weapons, less you count the rope coiled around the horse's neck.

They get within fifty yards and circle once, twice, makin' sure I'm as helpless as I appear. They yip and yell Indian curses at me, tryin' to get their courage up. When they get directly behind me, they charge. I start runnin' best I can, but of course the chains don't allow me to make much progress before they slam their horse into me, and knock me down. They jump off and attack me before I can get to my feet, but haven't counted on my ability to fight. I throw a fist at one of them and break his nose. He cries out and the other one stops in his tracks, but before he can back away, I grab him by the arm and pull him down beside me and and bust his cheekbone. He's young, and quick, and scrambles to his feet just in time to avoid gettin' seriously hurt. They retreat, screamin'. If it weren't for the fact they've been shamed, they'd probably give up and go home. But like I say, they're shamed.

Broken Nose calls the horse, climbs on, and gallops toward me. I get to my feet and start runnin' toward the stand of poplars. It's a long way, but if I can get there I'll be able to keep the trees between me and the horse, and create a standoff.

But these damn leg irons prove too cumbersome, and I get knocked down a second time. I decide to lie on the ground, figurin' the horse won't trample me if he comes at me again.

But I'm wrong.

The horse don't shy at all, and I barely avoided being crushed under its hooves. I jump to my feet and make one last effort to get to the trees. But my ankles are raw, and wet with blood, and every step feels like I'm stuck in quick sand.

I don't get far.

The third time he gallops toward me, I turn to face him, and raise my arms, plannin' to scream at the last minute to spook his horse. I'm hopin' he'll get bucked off, so I can knock him cold and stop this foolishness. But he reins his horse to a stop twenty feet from me, which gives Broken Cheekbone enough time to work his way behind me. He hurls a large rock that strikes the back of my head and knocks me loopy.

These young pups are dizzy and groggy from the punishment I gave them earlier, but they have the upperhand

and could easily kill me with the rock beside my head, a fact that's not lost on Broken Cheekbone, as he snatches it before I can.

But he don't use it to kill me.

Instead, he tucks the rock into a pouch attached to a wide strip of rawhide that circles his shoulder. It soon becomes clear why.

They want to torture me first.

They uncoil the length of rope from the horse's neck and loop the free end through one of my leg irons, and tie it. Then they drag me two hundred yards across the field on my back at a fast trot. They make a wide circle with me and drag me the other way. I can feel the grass burnin' and slicin' my neck and arms, and every now and then I hit some rocks, and it won't take too much more of this to kill me.

When they get to the other side of the field they turn to drag me again. There's no doubt they plan to drag me to my death, or nearly so, and then finish me off with the rock.

But then somethin' happens.

Broken Cheekbone falls off the back of the horse, unconscious. When he hits the ground, I grab him. Broken Nose abruptly stops the horse and slides off.

I don't want to kill these kids, but they've made it clear I'm in a life or death situation. As he starts walkin' toward me, I pull the rock from Broken Cheekbone's pouch. As Broken Nose looks on in horror, I crush his friend's skull.

Once again I'm responsible for killin' a kid.

And if Broken Nose comes a little closer, I'll kill him, as well.

But he's seen enough. He's afraid to leave his friend, but even more afraid not to. I see what's about to happen, so I pull the dead kid on top of me and hold on for dear life. Broken Nose jumps on the horse. When he digs his heels in to drag me to my death, the weight on our end is too heavy, and the rope breaks. The kid gallops off, dragging the broken rope behind him.

I don't know of too many sure things in this crazy world, but one thing I know for certain is Broken Nose will soon be back with half the tribe, which means I've probably got less than an hour to live.

I try to get to my feet, but fall unconscious. My eyes roll up into my head and I dream I'm bein' dragged across the field again.

My head starts to clear and I realize I'm not dreamin'. I actually *am* bein' dragged across the field! I lift my head and see Rudy in front of me. He's got a hold of my left leg and seems to be pullin' me back toward Dodge. Of course, my right leg is gettin' hung up under my body, and the pain is somethin' awful.

"Rudy!" I shout. "Stop! You're killin' me!"

Rudy hesitates, then stops, ambles over, and licks my face like a dog. Then he yawns, plops down beside me, and promptly falls asleep.

Just as I'm wonderin' how I came to have such bad luck, I see a horse, way off in the distance, headin' my way.

The Indians are comin'. They'll kill me, and Rudy, too.

"Rudy!" I scream. "*Run!*"

He's alert. He twitches his nose, pickin' up the scent.

"*Run!*" I shout. But Rudy has no intention of runnin'. He stands on his hind legs, throws his head back, and roars. I've heard this sound before, but never from Rudy. It appears whatever's headed toward us, we're goin' to face it together.

I reach around in the grass for the rock, find it, grip it tightly in my hand, and wait.

CHAPTER 9

WHAT SHOWS UP ain't a tribe of Indians. It's a lone white horse with no rider.

The horse is saddled, and there's a scabbard attached to it, with a rifle. There's two saddlebags that appear to be full, two canteens, and a large skinnin' knife. I blink twice, to make sure I'm not dreamin'.

I'm not.

I blink again anyway, 'cause it ain't every day you see a horse brave enough to walk right up to a wounded man and a bellowin' bear. While it goes against my grain to steal such a horse, I'd rather be hung tomorrow than scalped today, and this horse represents all I need to survive.

If I can get to my feet.

If I can get my leg over her back.

It ain't easy gettin' to my feet, 'cause my ribs are either bruised or broke, and my back feels wrenched. I get halfway up, hold myself there a second, take a deep breath, screw up all my strength, and finally stand on shaky legs. My breath is comin' out in a gaspy wheeze, and I'm worried I'm gonna scare the horse. But then I figure if she ain't afraid of the bear, my wheezin' sound ain't likely to affect her.

I hold my palm out and say, "Whoa, girl, whoa."

I take a step toward her. She don't shy away. I take a second step, and Rudy "tags" me and knocks me ass over heels while laughin' himself silly.

The horse laughs, too.

I ain't laughin'. I've got no strength left to stand. But then somethin' amazin' happens.

The horse walks right next to me and lies down!

All I have to do is get my leg over her back, and though it takes a pain-filled minute, I get it done.

The horse stands up, I remain on her back, and she starts headin' toward Dodge, with Rudy at our side. As we make our way steadily across the plain, I look from side to side for Indians. So far, so good. Of course, if they're gonna attack they'll come from behind us. I want to turn and look, but force myself not to, for fear I might fall.

Thirty minutes later, we're gettin' close to the field where I knelt this mornin', thinkin' about the picnic Gentry and I started that day in April, more than two years ago. Unfortunately, that means we're north of Dodge, and the horse is makin' no effort to turn south. I've regained enough of my strength to pull her mouth to the left, but she pays no attention. I pull harder, and she blows out a warnin' sound. While I appreciate her savin' my life, I need to be in Dodge, collectin' firewood. I feel bad that Rudy's got no tubers for supper, but he'll have to deal with it. I gather my strength and pull so hard the horse spins, and I fall off. She turns to look at me, then starts walkin' slowly in the direction she'd been takin' me when I fell.

I wave to the horse.

"Thanks for the ride!" I holler. I'm stronger now, and my head is clear. I'm hurt, but happy to be alive. I work myself up to a standin' position, and watch the horse and Rudy headin' west, even as I start walkin' south. I don't know this mare well enough to think any thoughts about her either way, but I'm surprised to see Rudy abandon me like this.

"So that's how it's gonna be, is it?" I holler, disgusted.

A short time later I hear a sound, and turn to see the horse and bear walkin' behind me, fifty yards back. Minutes later, they close to within five feet, and now we're walkin' single file: me, the mare, and the bear, which is how we walk through the town, and into the front door of my old saloon, the *Lucky Spur*.

At which point I remember the saddlebags.

I'm hurtin' so bad I can't remove the leather bags from the horse, but I can open 'em. I know the contents don't belong to me, but it's almost as if they do, since one of the bags is filled with tubers, and the other contains corn dodgers, pork cracklin's, and two hundred dollars in gold coins. That, plus the rifle, knife, and horse, represents a temptin' haul.

Too temptin'.

Like somethin' the devil might offer, to steal a man's soul.

I'll take the tubers for Rudy, and replace 'em when I can. The rest of the contents will stay where they are, in the saddlebag, 'cause they ain't mine to take. It'd be so easy to teach this brave horse how to turn south, and ride her all the way to Springfield, but I won't.

Last time I rode a horse I didn't buy it cost me twenty-eight months of hard time. I ain't about to repeat that mistake.

CHAPTER 10

IT'S MORNIN'.

I gathered no firewood yesterday, and hurt so bad I don't know how I managed to climb the steps. Guess I was that determined to sleep in my old bed. I'm lyin' here still, racked with pain. It's killin' me to lie here when there's wood to be gathered and a fire to be started so I can finally get these cursed chains off my ankles. But I have to accept things as they are. I'm lucky to be alive, and need to be content with that. Need to get myself healed before I start liftin' and carryin' large amounts of lumber.

Rudy's snout is nuzzlin' my leg. He slept on the floor by my bed last night, and seemed so comfortable doin' it, I figure Gentry must a' let him sleep here when she wasn't in the rockin' chair guardin' him.

I sigh, and the effort of doin' so makes me wince. I need to piss in the worst way, but dread the thought of gettin' up, goin' down the stairs to the outhouse, and climbin' back up. We used to have piss pots in each room, but now I ain't got a pot to piss in. The whores must a' made off with 'em last year when they cleared out.

I'm settin' my jaw against the pain, but pause to notice the lines of light comin' through the torn curtains, highlightin' the words and symbols on the wall. Emmett & Gentry. Two hearts. Emmett & Gentry. Two hearts.

I look at Rudy.

"Where's the horse?"

He stares at me, blankly.

"What'd you do, leave her downstairs?"

He opens his mouth like he's gettin' ready to answer, then peels his lips back and grins at me. I don't know if that's a smilin' expression or somethin' he does 'cause he feels like it. I ain't spent an abundance of time among black bear, and them I dealt with were stern-natured, so when it comes to smilin', it's Rudy's secret to know, and mine to find out.

I make my move to get out of bed and hear myself gasp with pain. I wouldn't a' thought it'd be harder to stand today than it was yesterday, but it is. When I finally make my way down the stairs, draggin' the chains behind me, the racket I make is enough to wake up what's left of the town.

I'm in the outhouse now, and somethin' don't feel right about the way I'm pissin'. The light comin' through the crescent moon at the top a' the door ain't givin' off enough light to see by, so I piss a little into my hand and hold it near a knot hole, and sure enough, there's blood in my piss. In my experience, that's never a good sign. I remember my witchy friend, Rose, tellin' me about coughin' up blood. One type of color is worse than another, and there was somethin' about smellin' copper, but I can't remember enough about it.

I do miss Rose, and all her knowledge of useful things.

Right now I could use some of the birch bark medicine she taught me how to make. If I'm pissin' this quantity of blood, and my ribs are busted or bruised, things could quickly go bad for me. There used to be a fine sawbones in town, but I doubt Doc Workday is still practicin' here. My guess is he ain't.

I push open the outhouse door and walk a few steps to the water trough. There ain't but a couple inches of water in it, and what's there is covered with a layer of green scum. There are mosquitoes standin' on it.

All in all, I'd say my hands are cleaner than the trough water.

I look at the pump handle. It's been a long time since I worked the pump, but back then it only took a couple minutes to draw. But that was April, and this is August. In my experience, August is about a five-minute pump, and I'm in such pain I doubt I could pump a single stroke. I look around to see if anyone is nearby who can lend a hand, but there ain't no one in sight.

I skitter the back of my hand across the scum on the water till I've made an open area big enough to put my hands in. I swirl 'em around a bit and wipe 'em on my pants.

I wonder if I'm bleedin' inside. Internal bleedin', is what Rose calls it, and you usually see blood comin' out of a person's mouth shortly before he dies.

Gentry had a friend, a whore named Scarlett, who got gored by a hydrophobic bull on the journey we made from Rolla to Dodge. She had the internal bleedin' Rose talks about, and sure enough, she died not long after the blood came out her mouth.

I take a minute to think about Scarlett. She weren't a pretty whore, but she was sturdy, hard-workin', courageous, and had a sunny disposition. Accordin' to Gentry, Scarlett was also uncommonly generous with her charms, which is the most useful quality a woman can have, in my opinion. Scarlett would've made a helluva pioneer wife after her whorin' days were done, had she lived long enough to find a decent man. She puts me in mind of Clara Bigsby, Jim's wife, 'cept I doubt Clara's as eager with her charms as Scarlett was said to be.

All these thoughts of Scarlett's internal bleedin' puts my mind on the blows I took to the back yesterday, and all the draggin' through the fields, and I come to the conclusion I ain't bleedin' on the inside. I figure it's a kidney bruise that's causin' the blood. Nonetheless, it'd be smart to boil some birch bark in water and drink it like a tea. It tastes somethin' awful, but it stops infection, inflammation, and helps a body heal quickly. If I drank three or four cupfuls between now and tomorrow, it'd probably heal my back as well as my kidneys.

I know where there's some birch, 'cause I used to cut it every week and drink the tea every day. But the birch I know is a good ways out of town.

Then again, I've got a horse in the saloon, less she run off durin' the night. If she's still here, I'll name her Scarlett.

Instead of walkin' back up the stairs to the bedroom, I walk around the buildin' and go in the front door.

Not only is Scarlett still here, she's still saddled. I feel bad about havin' left her that way since yesterday afternoon, but my pain was intolerable at the time, and it was all I could do to get up the stairs and climb into bed. I look at the two canteens hangin' on either side of the saddle horn and wonder if her owner would begrudge me a few swallows. If it were me, I'd offer the water, and a few corn dodgers to boot. I decide he's as generous as me, and help myself. Rudy hears me crunchin' corn dodgers and comes barrelin' down the stairs. I toss him one, which makes him need another. I toss him another, and that tastes like some more.

"These ain't ours, Rudy," I say, closin' the saddlebag.

Rudy bleats at me to show his displeasure.

"Behave," I say. "You've got tubers."

I toss him one.

He throws it back at me. When I duck out of the way, I feel a sharp pain stabbin' my hip. What the hell caused that one? Two minutes ago my hip was the only part of me that weren't in agony, and now it's the thing I'm feelin' most.

I sigh, and lead Scarlett outside so she can relieve herself. After she does, she gets on her knees and waits for me to climb on her back. I look around, to see if anyone's watchin' us. I don't want to be accused of stealin' another horse, but I could sure use that medicine.

I climb on Scarlett's back, and she takes off at a slow trot. Every step she takes is like the devil breakin' my bones and jugglin' 'em. I can't remember the last time I was in such pain, even when I was workin' on the railroad with swollen feet and infected ankles. Scarlett takes me due north, about three miles, at which point we come to the spot where I need to veer to the right if I'm gonna cut some birch bark. I guide her expertly to the right, only she don't go to the right. She's goin' due north. It finally dawns on me what's goin' on here.

Scarlett's tryin' to get home to her owner. If I'm right about that, her owner is another three miles north, and then west, which is the direction she was tryin' to force me yesterday when she threw me off her back.

I ain't about to be thrown again, so I remove the knife from its leather holder and tuck it into my pants. Then say, "Whoa, Scarlett." She stops, as if acceptin' her new name, lowers me to the ground, and I get off and start walkin' toward the birch trees.

"Thanks for the ride," I call out, cheerfully.

Two minutes later I turn to see her walkin' directly behind me. She follows me another mile, all the way to the birch trees.

I use the knife to cut about a pound's worth of bark, then look at Scarlett. She goes down to the ground again, and I climb back on. She takes me a mile due west, to the north-south trail, and turns right. If you'd a' told me you had a horse that can't make a left turn, I'd a' slapped you for bein' crazy. But this horse ain't made a left turn yet.

"Is it possible for you to take me back to town?" I say.

I try to ease her gently around, but she ain't havin' none of it.

I sigh. "Whoa."

Scarlett stops, lowers me to the ground. I get off and start walkin' toward town, and she soon falls in line behind me.

"You gonna make me walk the whole three miles?" I say.

Scarlett says nothin'.

"I ain't never had to walk so many miles with a saddled horse in my whole life," I say.

Scarlett remains quiet, just follows me at a distance of five feet, all the way back to Dodge.

CHAPTER 11

WHEN I FINALLY limp into town, Jim's standin' outside
the *Spur*.

"You waitin' for me?"

"I am for a fact."

"Somethin' wrong?"

"We were expectin' you for dinner last night."

"It's hot," I say.

"It is."

"Why not wait inside the *Spur*?"

"You might a' forgot there's a bear in there," he says.

"Rudy would never hurt you."

"So you say. But I'll keep my distance from a bear when
you ain't around, if it's all the same to you."

"He's partial to corn dodgers," I say.

Jim rubs his beard. "That's good to know. Where'd you get the horse?"

We go inside, and Scarlett follows us in.

"You won't believe this, but she just showed up yesterday, northwest of here."

"Where?"

"You know the poplar field, several miles out?"

"You're tellin' me you walked all the way to town yesterday mornin', then turned around and walked all them miles to a poplar field, draggin' them chains?"

"Had to get tubers for Rudy."

"What do you mean the horse just showed up? With a rifle, saddle, bags, blanket?"

"Yup. Any idea who her owner is?"

He gives Scarlett a long look. "I can't remember seein' a finer horse."

Jim ran a livery for fifteen years. I say, "Well, you'd know."

He nods. "Thought you'd be buildin' your blacksmith fire by now."

"I got laid up in my back."

"I could see you were limpin' pretty bad."

"Got bushwhacked by Indians."

Jim frowns. "How many?"

"Just two. Boys. But they gave me all I could handle."

"Due to the chains?"

I nod. "Had to kill one of 'em. Hurt the other one, but they still managed to hit me with a rock and drag me a bit."

"You're lucky to be alive."

"And that's the truth," I say.

We sit quiet a minute. Then he says, "You gonna keep the horse?"

"Ain't mine to keep."

"Have you ridden her, or does she just follow you around?"

"She only goes in certain directions. But left ain't one of 'em."

"*What?*"

"She don't make left turns."

Jim looks at me like I've lost my mind.

"When ridin' west," I add. "Nor right, while ridin' north."

Jim tries to squint my meanin'.

Aimin' for accuracy I say, "Left ain't right."

"Huh?"

"I mean, left ain't the right word. East is."

He appears more confused than ever. "East is what?"

"East is what she won't turn. Or south."

"The mare won't turn east or south?"

"Not in my experience."

Jim takes off his hat, shakes his head, puts it back on. I'm in too much pain to allow this conversation to continue much further. I try to explain myself one last time.

"The horse will carry me north out of town, but only to the Arkansas River. Then she'll go west. No amount of pullin' will get her to take any other direction."

"But she followed you into town."

"Ain't it the damndest thing you ever saw?"

"Maybe her owner lives west of the river."

"I was thinkin' that same thought."

"Maybe her owner's hurt and the horse come lookin' for help."

"She would've had to walk past a hundred folks on either side of the river at any given time," I say, "findin' me before noon as she did."

"Maybe she figured you're the only one that could help her owner."

"Who figured that," I say. "The horse?"

Jim shrugs.

Now it's my turn to look at him like he's crazy. Maybe we're both crazy. In any case, I'm done with this bullshit conversation. Time to change the subject.

"What've you got planned for the day?"

He points at my feet.

"What about 'em?"

"I'm available."

"For what?"

"To help you get them cuffs off. You're too hurt to do it yourself."

"I can't pay you. Not yet, anyway."

"Consider it an investment."

"In what?"

"Saving Dodge."

I frown. "You know I aim to find Gentry soon as I'm able to travel."

"You and Gentry need each other," Jim says, "but Dodge City needs you both."

I like the way he put that.

"I'll not forget what you've already done for me, keepin' an eye on the *Spur* all these months," I say.

"You'd a' done the same for me."

He's right.

"If you'll point out the wood you want me to tote to the fire pit, I'll go ahead and get started."

"Could you help me unsaddle Scarlett first? And then maybe pump a bucket of water? That way I can water her and Rudy, and boil some medicine bark for myself."

Jim's grinnin' at me.

"What?"

"That's her name," he says.

"Who's name?"

"The baby."

"What baby?"

"Yours, you dang fool! Your baby's name is Scarlett."

"Scarlett? You sure?"

"Yep, it just come to me. Her name is Scarlett Rose."

CHAPTER 12

AFTER RUDY AND Scarlett have their fill to drink, I boil a small pan of water, toss in the birch bark and cook it till it turns the color of brown I'm lookin' for. While it cools, I point out the wood for Jim to collect. He carries two stout chairs over to Tom Collins's fire pit, and I follow him there. Tom and two other men, and ten women, are standin' there to greet us. I know all of 'em, but only recognize a few at first, which is fair, since I'm pretty sure none of 'em recognize me.

"Be careful," Jim murmurs as we approach. "These women are hopin' for a husband."

Ten women in the same town without a man? Unheard of!

Used to be the other way around. I remember a time when men outnumbered women a hundred to one west of the Mississippi. For years I made a livin' bringin' whores and mail order brides from Rolla and Springfield to central and western Kansas. Back then, the homeliest, crankiest women were treated like princesses. Now, dreadful as I am, these ten women are lookin' at me the same way I looked at Scarlett the horse yesterday, when I considered her my only hope of survival.

"Good afternoon," sheriff, they say, one after the other. The two men are George Reed, and Art Carbunkle. George used to own G. *Reed's Feed & Seed*, and Art used to play piano for me at the *Spur*, till I shot holes in it and forbade music. That's because when music was played, Rudy danced. When we learned Rudy only danced 'cause he'd been tortured as a cub, we put a halt to it. This is the first time I'd seen Art since firin' him years ago, and the first time in my life I'd seen him sober. Truth be told, he looked a lot healthier when he was drunk.

"You okay, Art?"

"Consumption," he says.

I shake my head. "Sorry to hear it."

If Art ain't high on Dodge's list of eligible bachelors, George Reed is even lower. His entire body's the color of lead, and he smells like a man weaned on stink weed. Even in a skeleton town like Dodge has become, the saddest women won't tolerate the scent comin' off George. But I give him credit. Most folks who look and smell like this would take their own life.

Jim tosses the chairs into the fire pit and looks at the men.

52

"The sheriff's ribs are busted," Jim says, "and his back is wrenched. His ankles and feet are infected, and he's down in his hip. Emmett ain't said any of this, but it's clear enough to me. Will anyone lend a hand?"

Jane Plenty speaks up. "The women will help you directly."

Jim nods, and looks at me as if to say "I warned you." Then he turns and heads back to the *Spur* to fetch more wood. Art and George shuffle slowly behind him.

Tom Collins says, "This is gonna take some time. I'll come back outside when there's enough wood in the pit."

He hops back into his shanty, leavin' me to stand alone, facin' a line of women like a young man at a town dance.

There's fifteen feet of dirt between us, and the women ain't shy, but each comes at me a different way. They're respectful of each other, even friendly, but I remember a couple of 'em bein' holy terrors when the town was flush. I'm speakin' of Jane Plenty and Claire Murphy, who happen to be the first to walk across the dirt to say hello.

"Howdy Jane," I say, tippin' my hat as best I can, since it still hurts to raise my arm that high. "Claire," I add.

"Sheriff," Claire says. "I've got some liniment that might help you, if you want to come by later."

"Nice of you to offer," I say.

She nods, and steps back. What I remember about Claire, she wanted me to publicly flog the whores at Patty's Pie Palace for makin' lewd bathroom sounds at her and her friends when they walked to church one mornin'. Claire's one of the meanest proper women I ever encountered, so I doubt I'll be stoppin' by for liniment any time soon.

Jane's turn. She gives me a shy smile and whispers, "Emmett, you look like you could use some tending. I'm small, but sturdy. She starts to go, then turns back and takes two steps toward me, and leans close enough for me to smell the lilac in her hair. She whispers, "It's shameful and humiliating for us to throw ourselves at you like this, but we know you're a good man."

She takes a step back and looks me in the eye. "I'll admit I was a bit high and mighty when you were sheriff. But I've come down a peg. I'm a humble, warm-hearted woman who knows her place." She touches my arm, and keeps her hand there.

"What's become of Pete?" I say.

She shakes her head. "The war got him."

I nod. We both look at her hand a moment, and she gives my arm a little squeeze before removin' it. Then she steps back in line with the others. What I remember about Jane is seein' her small, freckly, left bosom when one of our whores ripped her blouse in my saloon one mornin'. Jane's husband was one of the few men in town who used to poke Leah, our most unfortunate-lookin' whore. In fact, Leah was the only whore Pete would poke, but he never said why, and I guess I'll never know.

The rest of the women come up to me, one-at-a-time, to re-introduce themselves. I'd seen Carol, Laurie, Gerta, and Louise a scant twenty-eight months ago, but all four appear to have aged ten or fifteen years.

Lilly Gee's the beauty of the bunch. She's twenty-two. Her husband, Al, was kicked in the head by a horse some years ago, such that he could only eat, shit, and hoot like an owl. Lilly stood by his side faithfully, despite the fact she was widely coveted by men of all ages for her backside, and it's as handsome as ever, from what I can tell. If she's in this line it means Al's finally passed on. Lilly nods at me from a distance, but declines smilin' or comin' closer. She probably showed up to see what I look like and don't think much of what she sees. I can't blame her for that. Nor would I care if she found me attractive, since I'm already spoken for. While Lilly don't have Gentry's looks, she's clear-faced and well-formed, and it says a lot about the state of things in Dodge for her to be without a man, her bein' right in the middle of her child-bearin' years.

Alice Crapper looks the same. I smile as she approaches, rememberin' how Gentry and I used to laugh about her name. She curtsies while sayin', "It's been awhile, Emmett. Hope you'll come visit me, if you plan to stay in town awhile."

"Thanks, Alice."

She winks, and tosses her hair like a schoolgirl as she spins around to rejoin the others. I put Alice's age at around thirty.

The last two, Margaret Stallings and May Gray, look at each other before Margaret decides to make her move. Margaret's a good ten years older than me, and was married to a gifted farmer named Will. Her son, Charlie, was seventeen last I saw him. Charlie got his first poke from a one-eyed whore I brought here from Rolla, Missouri, named Mary Burns. Mary used to tease Charlie somethin' unmerciful in public, but had a soft spot for the boy and often allowed him to dip in her well for little or no charge.

"How's Burt?" I ask.

Margaret don't respond. Just stares blankly, like she's thinkin' other thoughts.

"Charlie?" I say.

She looks at me with a grim face that's tryin' to force a smile, but two quick tears tell the story. They spill out her eye and run down her cheek. She don't bother whisperin', just says, "I'm available, Emmett," and says nothin' further.

Last one up is May Gray. Savin' her comments for last, so I'll remember 'em first. May approaches and says, "Walk with me a few steps, Emmett."

I turn and we walk till we're far enough away that the others can't hear.

"Earl got himself killed, like all the others," she says.

"I'm sorry to hear that, May."

"We're all in pain, Emmett. But in some ways, yours is worse, because you don't know what Gentry's done yet."

I snap to attention. "What do you mean? Do you know something?"

May looks at the women behind her, then back at me, and says, "I have some information, but I can't tell you here, in front of everyone."

"Why not?"

"Gentry and I had a conversation. But she made me promise not to tell anyone about it."

I never knew Gentry and May to be close enough to share secrets. May's husband, Earl, used to drive dead bodies to Fort Dodge to be buried, and he frequented the saloon regularly, but Gentry barely knew May, and they never spoke publicly or privately, to my knowledge.

"Why would Gentry put you in her confidence, 'stead of Jim and Clara?" I ask.

"It's true Gentry was partial to Jim and Clara. But I don't think she wanted them to know her plans."

"Why not?"

"I don't know, Emmett. But if she did, she would've told them. And she didn't."

May has three young children at home, and has always treasured her house and garden. Her father owned valuable property in St. Louis, and used to send her provisions on a regular basis. I assume he's still doin' so, if she's happy raisin' her kids in a ghost town.

"How are your girls?" I say, tryin' to be cordial.

"They're fine, thanks for asking. And no trouble at all! On the contrary, they're quite helpful to have around the house. All three can milk, churn butter, and sew. The oldest is a fine cook, and the youngest has a voice like a songbird. The middle one's strong as an ox, and can prime a pump and carry two buckets of water all the way from the crick without stopping."

"That must be nice for you."

She nods.

I say, "When can we talk?"

"Come to my house tonight at eight. I'll cut your hair and smooth your face and tell you the small bit I know about your Gentry."

"I'll be there," I say.

CHAPTER 13

WHEN THE WOMEN pitch in to help, George and Art are thankful to quit workin', and head home, before somethin' else can be asked of 'em. These women are of strong pioneer stock, and ain't afraid of work. Even Lilly, who ain't interested in me, is workin' up a sweat. It takes about an hour to get enough wood to set the five fires Tom Collins says will last us the rest of the day. The women watch Tom light the fire, and stick around till my screamin' starts.

I knew it'd hurt, but the surprise is how much. We start right in with the cuffs instead of the chains, 'cause I don't want to waste an extra two to four days. Jim handles the poker. When he presses it against the cuff around my leg, bits of sparks fly onto my skin and burn it. As he presses the poker harder, more sparks fly, and the cuff starts gettin' hot. So hot that the wet cloth I've wrapped between my ankle and the cuff starts to smoke with steam. Seconds later it's almost as hot as the poker, and the heat is comin' through the cloth and boilin' the open wounds in my ankles and feet. I dip some more water onto the cloth, and it sends a shower of steam so thick I can't see my foot for several seconds. When the poker cools off, Jim pulls it away, and we inspect the cuff.

There's an ash-gray circle on it, but no dent.

No dent whatsoever.

He looks at me and shakes his head.

"It's a process," I say. "Let's light the next one."

It goes like that all afternoon, and my whole body feels like it's on fire. First, it's August, and the heat is considerable. Second, I've been sittin' by a roarin' fire all afternoon. Third, I feel like my whole body's infected on the inside from the beatin' I took yesterday. Fourth, the bark medicine I drank has upset my stomach somethin' awful. That's a process, too, and one I've been through. It takes about three days for the birch bark to do its magic. Before my capture, I drank it every day, and it kept me from catchin' all the colds and other sicknesses the travelers brought with 'em to Dodge in them days. But that medicine'll give you the trots the first two days you drink it.

When the poker has cooled for the fifth time and my yelps have died down, Jim pulls the poker away, and just like the other four times, there's a burn mark.

But no dent.

"Ain't gonna work," Jim says.

"It takes time," I say. "Are you available tomorrow?"

He lifts his shirt tail and wipes the sweat from his face. "I'm good for maybe one more day," he says. "But at this pace, it'll take every last piece of wood from your saloon to get these chains off. And then where will you be?"

"I can rebuild, if I gotta. But these chains are a lot less fun than they look."

He says, "I feel for you, Emmett."

"I got it easy compared to most," I say.

We shake hands, and he leaves. I remain seated another half hour, not darin' to move till the cuff is no worse than warm to the touch. While I wait I think about Gentry, and the things that happened today. I wonder what May knows, and how reliable her information might be. It's a promisin' thought, but I don't get my hopes up about it.

Mainly I think about the ten women, and how far they've fallen the past twenty-eight months. They're humbled, but not beaten or broken. They're survivors. Even the strong-willed, harsh-tempered ones, like Claire and Jane showed a soft side today, and a willingness to work in the heat, and splinter their hands and backs and shoulders carryin' heavy loads of wood in the stiflin' heat. It only took 'em an hour to haul what we needed for the fire, but I've got every reason to believe they would've stayed all day if such had been necessary.

I shake my head, thinkin' how I'd failed to appreciate these proper pioneer women. I never cared for their stern, churchy nature, and how they looked down on whores, and railed against pretty much everythin' that makes a man happy, like fuckin', drinkin', fightin' and gamblin'. But when

when it's all said and done, it was the husbands and sons who run off to shoot their kinfolk, and the whores, cowboys, drinkers, and card players—the folks I always liked—who gave up on the town and cleared out. The only ones courageous enough to stay here and try to carve out a life are the tough, stern, pioneer women, and their small crop of kids who'll be raised to be just as tough and useful as their ma's.

I think about what May Gray said today. Not about Gentry, but about her children. How the oldest one's a helluva cook and the youngest has a voice like a songbird, and the middle one's strong as an ox and can prime a pump. I could've used her today to get the water I needed. The whores can pump water, of course, but most of 'em rely on men to do the pumpin', and what other labor needs doin'. May said all three of her girls can sew, milk, and churn butter. Said they're hard workers and useful to have around. Reason I'm thinkin' these thoughts, none of the whores—not even Gentry—could cook any part of a decent meal. They didn't do their mendin' or even their own laundry. Sure, they were talented and helpful in other ways, but not in the ways that make a town survive, or help children learn useful skills.

Today I gained a new respect for these pioneer women, and resolve to make an attempt to be more tolerant of their naggy, bitchy, preachy ways.

CHAPTER 14

I'M HEADIN' BACK to the *Spur* when I realize it's gettin' close to eight. I don't want Jim to know how upset I am about how little we accomplished today, but in my heart I'm terribly discouraged.

I make fast work of feedin' Scarlett and Rudy, and give 'em some water while I'm drinkin' bark tea. The only thing liftin' my spirits is whatever news May might have to share about Gentry. The good news is I'm no longer pissin' blood, so I don't have internal bleedin'. I'm happy about that, but my thoughts are on Gentry more than anythin' or anybody else, so after takin' Rudy and Scarlett outside to relieve themselves, I head for May Gray's house, though I know I'm a few minutes early.

May shows a warm smile as she opens the door.

"Why Emmett, you're early!" she says.

"I hope that's not a problem."

"Of course not. Please, come in the parlor and make yourself comfortable."

"Don't mind if I do."

"Would you like a lemonade?"

"A...*lemonade?*"

"Do you not partake of sweet drinks?"

"Well, yes ma'am, I do. It's just...I ain't had a lemonade since I was a boy."

"And did you enjoy the experience?"

"I did indeed. But how did you come by lemons?"

"My father sent us two bags of lemons, and some coffee. We shared them with the town ladies, so you might have several chances to drink lemonade or coffee this week." She goes to the staircase and calls, "Girls? We have a guest. Come say hello."

I hear gigglin', then the sound of runnin' feet, and now three girls are standin' before me, tallest on the left, shortest on the right. The girls are fresh-scrubbed, well-scented, and wearin' clean dresses. The younger two have bows in their hair. I remember May used to strip the clothes off the dead bodies before Earl carted 'em off to Fort Dodge to be buried. I knew her to be a fine seamstress, and a woman who enjoyed hostin' the occasional dinner party.

"Introduce yourselves, ladies," May says.

From right to left they are Ellie, Grace, and little Molly. Ellie's ten, Grace is eight, Molly's five. They smile and curtsy while introducing themselves. When they're finished, I say, "You look beautiful, ladies," and the younger ones giggle.

Ellie ain't quite as friendly, but she's pleasant. Probably worried I'm here to take her Daddy's place.

"Would you care for some lemonade, Mr. Love?" Ellie says.

"If it ain't no bother," I say.

As she heads to the kitchen I think about how this sweet little girl is only ten, and yet she's the same age most of our whores were when they were forced into the business. Gentry herself was only two years older than Ellie when her parents sold her to a whore house in Jefferson City, Missouri. By the time I met her, she was seventeen, and had made her way to Rolla, tryin' to save up enough money to head west.

I got nothin' against whorin', if a woman's a certain age, like sixteen or older. But when a girl is ten or twelve, which the law allows, that's an injustice. The thought of grown men plowin' into these children's privates makes me see red. When I'm in a respectable settin' like this, where I can see the results of good parentin' like what May has done with these kids, I feel sorry for the sufferin' our whores experienced in their youth. I don't know how Gentry and the others managed to keep a happy disposition after what's been done to them. I'm reminded of how an hour earlier I was thinkin' badly about the whores for not learnin' how to cook and sew. But how could they have learned them things and other social graces while bein' forced to give up their childhoods? Now that I think on it, I realize with regard to proper women and whores, one kind a' woman ain't no better or worse than another, and there's somethin' good to be said for all of 'em. Mostly, I'm happy for parents like May, who love their children, and want to protect 'em, and are willing to teach 'em how to make a home.

While I'm drinkin' lemonade, May has little Molly sing a couple of hymns. When she's done I say, "That was right lovely, Molly. You've got a beautiful voice, and that's a fact."

She beams, curtsies, and points at my leg irons.

"*Molly!*" Ellie scolds.

"It's all right," I say. "She wouldn't be normal if she didn't wonder about 'em."

May says, "Girls, Mr. Love was captured by the Union Army, put in chains, and forced to work on a railroad. He's been at the blacksmith's shop all afternoon trying to burn them off. Any luck with that, Emmett?"

"No ma'am," I say.

She frowns. "That must be terribly discouraging."

"It is. But I ain't givin' up."

"No, of course not. And I'll be proud to help you with the wood tomorrow."

"Thank you."

"Not at all," she says, smilin'.

"Do they hurt?" Grace says.

"They're more of a nuisance than anythin' else."

"I don't know how you stand it," she says. "They'd make me crazy."

I smile at how such a grown up sentence can flow so smoothly from such a young girl. Then Ellie shows her considerable cipherin' skills by recitin' her times tables. When she gets to her sixes, I say, "I'm trustin' you to be honest from here on out."

She laughs and goes all the way to twelve times twelve, which she claims is a hundred and forty-four. I look at May.

"She's right," May says.

Then all three girls have a short conversation in French, and May has me call out some random words to see if her girls know how to say 'em in French. They didn't know "gunslinger" or "dynamite," but surprised me by gettin' "outhouse" and "stagecoach."

May's got a nice little family here, and it's clear her children mean the world to her. I s'pect no matter how bad things get, she'd never sell any of 'em to a whorehouse.

May tells Ellie to warm up some dinner for me.

"I don't want you to go to any trouble," I say. "I've got some corn dodgers back at my place."

"Nonsense," she says. "You'll have beefsteak and peas, and rhubarb pie, just as we did, earlier tonight."

"Rhubarb pie?"

"Finest in the county."

I want to ask about havin' steak, peas and pie when others in town are eatin' horsemeat, but I suppose May can't be expected to share everythin' her father sends. I also want to ask about Gentry, but don't want to appear rude. May knows why I came, and she'll get to the point eventually. In the meantime, it won't hurt to have my first decent meal in more than two years, and possibly a shave and a haircut, if she was serious about that part earlier today.

Within minutes I'm sittin' at the kitchen table, tuckin' into a thick slice of beef, while the girls wait on me, pourin' water, and settin' this plate down and pickin' that one up. I find the steak tender and tasty, as good as I've had in any restaurant. There were biscuits, too, and field peas picked fresh from her garden.

"These are the best field peas I ever tasted," I say.

"Why Emmett," May says, showin' me her warmest smile. "Thank you for saying that!"

"Well, it's true."

As dusk turns to dark, May says, "You girls go on up to your room, now, and keep the door closed. Mr. Love and I have some grown up things to discuss."

CHAPTER 15

GRACE AND MOLLY curtsy and tell me goodnight, and scamper upstairs. Ellie lingers until May gives her a warnin' look. Then Ellie says, "Goodnight, Mr. Love. It's been a pleasure meeting you."

"Goodnight, Ellie. You, too."

When May's comfortable the girls are locked away for the night, she serves me a slice of rhubarb pie. I eat it so fast she laughs out loud. After my second piece of pie, she sets a bucket of water behind my chair and slides another chair behind the bucket. Then she gets out a razor, a comb, and a pair of scissors, and ties an apron around my neck and fans it out behind me. Then says, "Oops."

"Oops?"

"I forgot you can't reach behind you to hold the apron."

She stands and says, "Hold still a minute." Then leaves the kitchen, goes to the base of the stairs in the hallway and calls for Ellie. Moments later, Ellie is standing behind me, holding the apron out to catch all the hair May is cutting. When she finishes my hair, she has Ellie hold the apron beneath my chin, and uses the scissors to cut most of my beard and mustache off.

When that's done, May sends Ellie back upstairs. Then she takes the apron outside for a few minutes. When she comes back in, it's folded. She places it back in the drawer where she'd got it earlier, then soaps my face and begins stropping the razor. When she's happy with the edge, she shaves me as expert as any barber ever has, and doesn't nick me but twice. Both cuts are very small, and only occurred at the corners of my nose. She apologizes all over herself, and says she's usually much better than this, but she's out of practice, and it won't ever happen again.

"May, that's as good a shave as I've ever had," I say.

"Well, I did cut you twice."

"Both times were my fault."

"Sweet of you to say."

She washes my face with a wet towel, then dries it and steps back to survey her work.

"You look ten years younger," she says.

"I believe it. Thank you."

We're both quiet a minute while May puts her things away and washes out her pail. Then she says, "I know you want to hear what Gentry told me."

"I do."

"It's not much, and I don't know if it'll prove helpful. But I'll tell you, directly. Before I do, I wonder if you'll allow me to ask you a few questions."

"Of course."

"You've always been an honest man, far as I can tell."

"I try hard to be."

"And a generally decent man, though you've consorted with prostitutes your entire life."

"Yes, ma'am."

"When you weren't killing men in the streets, or beating them senseless."

"Yes ma'am."

"Or plying decent town men with alcohol, and enticing them to gamble and fornicate with loose women of low moral character, despite the fact these men were married and made promises before the Lord."

I'm workin' hard to practice my plan to be more tolerant of proper women, knowin' their naggy, bitchy ways helps raise good-mannered, useful children and keeps towns alive when others leave. But I ain't had much experience bein' told off in such a casual way before, and don't know how long her list of things is that *don't* make me a generally decent man, so I say, "You had some questions for me?"

"I do. But they might give you pause."

"Why's that?"

"You might hesitate to be honest, in an effort to spare my feelings."

"That would be the gentlemanly thing to do," I say.

"Not in this case. I hope you'll be willing to tell me the truth, regardless of how it might make me feel."

"Okay."

"Do you promise?"

"To answer truthfully?"

"Yes."

"I promise."

She nods. "Good. Because I'm counting on your honesty."

"Ask your questions, May."

She takes a deep breath and says, "My husband, Earl."

"What about him?"

"I know he played cards at the *Spur.*"

"He did."

"And I know he drank."

"He did."

She pauses. While she does, I think about May's husband, Earl. The thing I remember most about him is he couldn't keep his dick in his pants. He went from one whore to the next. He'd fuck one, then another, then go back and fuck the first one again, all in the same night. He even fucked Leah, when the others were busy.

May's ready to speak. Before she does, she looks me deep in the eyes. Then says, "Did he have a particular favorite among the whores?"

"Earl?"

"Yes, Emmett," she says. "I'm asking about Earl."

"Why, Earl didn't visit the whores at all, May."

"Well, of *course* he did!"

"Not to *my* knowledge. And I ought to know."

Her bottom lip starts tremblin' slightly. "You're positive?"

"Completely. He never visited the whores, and they knew to leave him alone."

She looks down at the table.

I say, "The thing about whores, if they know a man ain't interested, they won't trouble him about it. They'd rather spend time with a likely prospect."

I notice she's cryin' softly.

"What's the matter?" I say. "It's a good thing, right?"

She looks up at me with moist eyes. "It's a very good thing. Except..."

"Except what?"

"I can't tell you how many nights he'd come home, smelling of rose water and perfume. We fought about it all the time. I was certain he was fornicating."

She cries some more. Harder, this time. I reach out and pat her hand.

"It ruined our relationship," she says.

"No it didn't," I say. "If it had, he would've spent time with the whores."

"I didn't allow him to touch me the last four years of his life."

Earl died a year ago. I cipher it out in my head, and say, "What about Molly?"

"The seed that created her was the last I took from that man."

"Well, I know he loved you."

She cries again, and this time I don't interrupt. Sometimes a woman needs a good cry. After cryin' herself out, she says, "I feel terrible."

"Why?"

"For treating him so badly. I'd feel better if he'd been fornicating all those years. I really would."

"You don't mean that," I say.

She looks up at me again. "No, of course not." She dabs at her eyes with a handkerchief that has suddenly appeared in her hand. While I try to figure out how she come by a handkerchief in such short order, she says, "I just wish I'd been a better wife."

I give the handkerchief a careful look, then wave my hand, indicatin' the house, and her life in general. "May, you've kept a beautiful, clean house, and a productive garden. You cooked and cleaned and mended for this man, and cared for him when he was sick. You birthed three beautiful girls, and educated them, and taught them skills that'll make 'em wonderful wives and mothers. And on top of all that, you were a good enough wife to keep your man from strayin' the entire time I knew him. Even all them last years, when he wasn't, uh...*couplin'* with you."

"You think he died happy?"

"I s'pect he died a happy husband and father."

"Thanks, Emmett."

"I'm only sayin' what's true, May."

"Well, thank you for that. I hope you'll continue telling the truth when I ask my next question."

CHAPTER 16

"EMMETT?" MAY SAYS.

"Huh?"

"Do you promise to answer my next question truthfully?"

"I do. Ask it."

"There were ten of us women in that line today," May says.

I nod.

"I know your only interest is Gentry, at this time."

"That's true."

"I'm aware if you find Gentry, if she still wants you, everything will be fine."

"It will."

"I hope it goes the way you want it to."

"Thanks, May."

"You're welcome."

I pause. "Was that your question?"

"No. What I was wonderin'..."

"Which of you I'd choose if Gentry weren't in the picture?"

"Yes. I mean, I know you'd want Lilly, of course. She's young, beautiful, and has no children to get in your way. She'd be your first choice without question."

"She would, I s'pect. For all them reasons you said."

May nods. "Thank you for being honest."

"I said I would be."

"You did." Then she says, "But Lilly's not interested in you."

"I gathered that."

"She thinks you're too old. And questions your morals."

"She's probably right on both counts."

"Well, like I say, she's young. She hasn't learned there aren't any perfect men in the world. No offense."

"None taken."

"So that leaves nine," she says.

"It does."

She bites her lip and says, "Do you find me attractive at all, Emmett?"

I rub my chin, ponderin' the best way to answer, and get a surprise, havin' forgotten what a smooth chin feels like.

I say, "I'll be honest with you, May."

She looks at me with what appears to be a sudden sadness in her eyes.

"There was only one of the nine I'd a' put in front of you before tonight."

"Just one?"

"Just one."

"Who?"

"It ain't important."

"It is to me. Is it Alice Crapper?"

"No."

"Are you sure about that? She's five years younger than me, and flirtier, and Alice told us you've always had a crush on her."

That surprises me, and May can see it in my face.

"It's not true?" she says.

"I don't mind her thinkin' that, if it's what she wants to think."

My words seem to please her, but then she scrunches her lips to one side and says, "I can't see you with Jane. Or Claire."

"I was leanin' toward Margaret," I say.

"*Margaret?* But she's so..."

"Old?"

"Well...I'm just surprised after bein' with Gentry, who was what back then, seventeen?—that you'd switch to a woman who's nearly fifty! Why choose Margaret over the rest of us?"

"Margaret appears to be barely hangin' on. If I ever lost Gentry's love, I'd be no more'n a shell of a man, with almost nothin' to offer a woman. But what little I had left might bring comfort to a woman who understands my loss and feels the same way."

"Why Emmett, that's beautiful."

"It is?"

"In a sad, depressing way, yes."

"Thank you."

"Before tonight," she says.

"Excuse me?"

"When you answered my question you said before to-night you would've put one of the nine women ahead of me. Does that mean you've changed your mind about Margaret?"

"No. It means I changed my mind about you."

"Really?"

I nod.

"Tell me," she says.

I think a minute, figurin' out how best to put it in words. I finally come up with, "It's everything I've seen here tonight. What you've done with your life. Your girls. Your devotion to your house, and your town."

"Tell me, Emmett."

"You're makin' the best of a terrible situation, and doin' it with style and grace, from what I can see. You're a bit preachy for my taste, and I think you'd be quick to nag at me. I don't think you'd shy away from pointin' out my shortcomin's, neither."

"But?"

"But you're a good woman, and a wonderful mother. You're independent. A givin' person. If I felt there was any life worth livin' without Gentry in it—which I doubt—then it'd likely be with a woman like you, who don't give up when things go sour. I'd need the type a' woman who has positive thoughts and can carve a pleasant life from the worst circumstances."

May's smilin' very warmly, which tells me I'm sayin' all the right things, like when I lied about Earl not consortin' with our whores. I'm hopin' this friendly talk will earn me another slice of rhubarb pie."

May says, "It's been almost six years for me."

"Huh?"

"Six long years since I've enjoyed the close company of a man."

I nod. "That's a long time. A woman like you probably has a lot of love to give the right man."

"So if Gentry's moved on and no longer wants you?"

"I'd have to go through a terrible period before havin' thoughts of bein with another woman."

"Yes, of course. But wouldn't it be comforting to know there's someone else in the world who'd love to have you if that awful thing happens? Even if that person had a history of being a preachy, nagging woman?"

"That'd be a good thing to know. But I'm countin' on Gentry wantin' me."

"You've been very patient with me," May says, "and I'll tell you my news about Gentry very soon. Will you do me the favor of turning your head first, for just a moment?"

I turn my head and hear her walk out of the room, which gives me time to wonder if there's any pie left. A half minute later, I hear her come back in.

"You can turn your head back now," she says.

When I do, I almost faint from shock. May Gray is standin' before me stark naked!

I jump to my feet and give out a loud groan.

"Oh, Emmett," she says. "You've been so long without a woman!"

What? Does she think I'm groanin' for sex?

I'm not!

I'd been so startled, I forgot my injuries. I'm gaspin' from the pain of bangin' into the side of the table just now, not her nakedness! But I don't want to hurt her feelin's. Specially after feedin' and shavin' me, and cuttin' my hair. I'm confused how things got to this point. One minute I'm thinkin' about rhubarb pie, now I'm bracin' myself against the table, as May moves closer.

"May—"

"Shhh!" she says, and before I know what's happenin', she's kissin' me, and her hand is suddenly inside my baggy pants, and somehow she's loosened the rope I was usin' for a belt. I feel my pants slidin' down my legs, and she's gropin' around, reachin' for...

"Do you find me attractive at all, Emmett?" she says, as my pants fall to my ankles and her hand finds what it was searchin' for.

"I—"

"Do you find me attractive at *all?*" she gasps, and starts strokin' and pullin' on me. One of my arms is headin' skyward without any help from me. My arm shouldn't be able to do that without a tremendous amount of pain, but for some reason I don't feel it at all, and now I realize my head is lookin' upward too, and my mouth is wide open, makin' silent screamin' sounds. I'm tryin' to make my brain understand that what's happenin' ain't supposed to be happenin', but it's like my brain has gone somewhere else and all that's left is a feelin' I ain't felt in a helluva long time. This ain't somethin' I wanted to happen, but it sure enough *is* happenin', and I'm tryin' to think of the right words to say, and they ain't comin' to my lips, but I finally force my mouth to gasp "*Gentry!*"

"I *know*," May says. "You love Gentry. I bet you love it when Gentry does *this!*"

She pulls me toward her, and when I realize what she's tryin' to do, I almost laugh out loud because there's no way she can get me inside her from this angle. But then she amazes me by hikin' her leg on top of the table. I take a split-second to marvel at her bendability, 'cause that's somethin' you wouldn't expect a proper woman to even *think* of, much less *do*. It's clear at this point May ain't got the skills to match a seasoned whore, but she's much more determined, and that counts for plenty. In fact, she's so close to achievin' her goal, I have to jump back to keep from cheatin' on Gentry, though I suppose a critical observer might accuse me of havin' crossed that line already.

"Take me, Emmett!" she gasps.

I put my hand out to hold her back, but she grabs it to her breast.

"I won't say a word," May says. "It'll be our secret!"

"I can't."

"You can! You *are!*"

Am I? I look down. No, I'm not. But I'm close.

"May," I say, firmly. "Stop."

"Huh?"

"Stop."

She backs away, starts to cry.

Shit.

"I'm too fat," she says.

"You ain't fat at all!" I say.

"I'm too *skinny? Really?*"

"No."

"Oh."

"It's my stretch marks. You hate them. Oh, God, I'm so embarrassed."

"It ain't you," I repeat.

"I'm too hairy. You've been with those young harlots so long, I've frightened you."

Now that she mentioned it, I see she *is* uncommonly hairy. But it didn't frighten me till just now. She sees me starin at the hair coverin' her nipples, and the thick patch of hair between her breasts. But she ain't moved away yet. I think she's wonderin' if I'm changin' my mind. The proper thing would be to turn away, but I can't. Lookin' at her titties is like watchin' twin calves bein' born. It ain't a pretty sight, but you can't stop starin'.

May's no longer cryin'. She's grinnin'. But I don't know why.

"You *like* them!" she says.

"Huh?"

"This is what a real woman looks like, Emmett. And you *like* it, I can tell."

I have no idea what she's talkin' about till she points at the part of me she grabbed earlier, and I realize the little amount of attention I received is still havin' an effect.

"Let's finish what we started," she says. "It's a natural thing."

"I can't."

"Looks to me like you can," she says, gigglin'.

"Well, like I say, it ain't you, and I guess this is the proof."

"That's well put," she says, "under the circumstances."

She gives out a big sigh, leaves the room to put her clothes back on. I try to reach down to pull up my pants, but my back has locked up and I can't bend that far. I lean one hand on the table and try to lift my opposite leg, hopin' to get enough material in my hand to pull my pants up the rest of the way, but the weight of the leg irons makes the pain unbearable. There's nothin' to do but stand here like an idiot and wait for May to come back in and pull my pants up.

Unfortunately, when she's dressed, she goes to the stairwell before enterin' the kitchen and yells, "Girls? Come downstairs and say goodbye to Mr. Love."

CHAPTER 17

I HEAR THE door open upstairs. One of the girls says, "Did you call us?"

May says, "Come on down and say goodnight to Emmett."

While that's happenin', I try again to pull up my pants, but my back simply ain't allowin' it. This is all I need, to be standin' here naked from the waist down with my pants around my ankles and have May and her girls walk in!

I hear the girls on the landin' upstairs, and throw myself on the floor and bend my legs toward my chest. It's workin', but I hear the girls thumpin' down the stairs already, which means I ain't gonna make it!

I roll under the kitchen table, while pullin' fiercely on my pants. Just as they enter the kitchen, I get the pants up, but can't tie the rope belt. I lay there very quietly, tryin' to work the rope, but it's caught in the chains on my leg irons. I can't reach that far, but I have one end of the rope belt in my hand.

"Mr. Love?" Ellie says.

I'm fumblin' with the rope belt. Next thing I know, little Molly has spied me on the floor, under the table.

"He's under the table!" she squeals.

May enters the kitchen, says, "Emmett, what on earth are you doing on the floor?"

I say, "My back was lockin' up. I needed to stretch it out."

"You picked just now to do that?"

"I did. A spasm come over me just as you called for the girls."

"Well, let me help you up."

"No!"

The minute I stand, my pants will fall back down around my ankles!

"I know it's terrible rude," I say, "But if you don't mind, I'd like to lay here a little longer. Girls, I feel bad not to stand and give you a proper good evenin'. But this old back of mine has put me in a dither."

The four females stand where they are. I suppose they're lookin' at each other, tryin' to figure out what to do, and finally May has them say goodnight from where they are. I answer from where I am, and she sends them back upstairs. When they're back upstairs, she gets on her hands and knees and looks under the table and says, "What's really going on?"

By the time I tell her, she's laughed herself silly.

Once I'm finally on my feet with my belt secure around my waist, I say, "Can you please tell me what Gentry shared with you?"

We walk outside and stand on her front porch. It's a hot, muggy night, and the crickets in the garden behind her house are making a steady buzzin' sound. When a moth gets hung up in May's hair she flails away at it till she's satisfied it's gone. Then she says, "This is a bad idea. Let's go back inside."

I follow her in and close the door. As I turn to face her she says, "Here's the thing, Emmett. Gentry's run off with a cattleman from England."

CHAPTER 18

MY STOMACH LURCHES. I fall back against the door as if I'd been pushed. For some reason I don't understand, I take a few steps forward, and grab the beam in the center of May's parlor, to keep from fallin' down.

"I'm so sorry, Emmett," May says.

"What cattleman?"

"He first showed up Christmas before last, a couple months before the rebels robbed the bank."

"The bank was robbed?"

"Jim didn't tell you?"

"No."

"That's the main reason the stores shut down. Most folks had their life's savings in the bank, and got wiped out financially. The stores lent as much credit as they could, but had no cash to restock their inventories. So all the men folk above thirteen signed up to soldier. It was the only paycheck available."

I heard her words, but couldn't focus on 'em. I remember Jim Bigsby mentioned somethin' about the English cattleman who taught Gentry about Christmas trees. But if Gentry ran off with him, Jim didn't seem to know about it.

"When you say Gentry ran off with this man, what do you mean? Did she tell you she was going with him?"

"Do you want to sit down?"

"No. I want you to tell me exactly what Gentry told you."

May pauses, then says, "Well, Gentry only spoke to me once. It was evening, and she was walking very quickly on the street boards, on her way back to the *Spur*, and when she turned the corner, she ran right into me and knocked me down. When she helped me up I could see she was crying."

My hands become fists.

May continues, "I asked her what was wrong. At first she didn't want to say. Then she told me the Englishman had come back to get her."

"What do you mean?"

"Apparently he'd become smitten with her the first time they met, and he snuck back into town several times to meet her. He proposed to her, and promised a better life for her and the baby."

"And she said yes?"

"According to Gentry, she said no. Then she made me promise not to tell anyone about our conversation. But the next morning she and the baby were gone, and no one's seen them ever since. It makes sense they went with the Eng-lishman to his cattle ranch."

"Where's the ranch?"

"I honestly don't know."

I pace from the post to the door, then back.

"Why do you think she was cryin'?"

"I couldn't say for certain."

"What's your belief?"

"Looking at it purely from a mother's viewpoint, I think Gentry didn't love him. But he was rich and she was broke, and couldn't provide for her baby. A woman who loves her child will do whatever it takes to keep her child safe."

My heart hurts, thinkin' about Gentry bein' forced to make such a terrible decision.

"She met this man before Christmas, and kept the Spur open another three months," I say.

"That sounds about right."

"When did the bank get robbed?"

"End of January, 1862."

"And she stayed at the *Spur* another year?"

"I don't know, Emmett. Gentry and I weren't very close. We only had the one conversation, and she was quite upset at the time."

I nod, while forcin' my brain to understand what's hap-pened. I always knew at some point Gentry was likely to run off with a younger, more handsome man. If that's what's happened, I'll want to hear it from her lips.

"What's this Englishman's name?" I ask.

May shakes her head. "I don't know. I'm sorry, Emmett, I truly am. Maybe Jim can tell you more about him. I think they shared a few drinks together."

"You never said anythin' to Jim or anyone else about what Gentry told you?"

"No, of course not! I'm not a teller of secrets. I'm only telling *you* because I know you're in love with her, and want to find her."

I look her in the eyes. "You also want me to choose you."

She looks down at the floor, and says "Yes." Then she looks back up at me and adds, "But only if Gentry spurns you."

"Say exactly what you mean."

She sighs. "Emmett, I won't give my heart and home to a man who's undecided about me. I want you to find Gentry, and see if she wants to be rescued. If she does, I'll be very happy for you, and if you choose to live in Dodge City, you and I can pretend that tonight never happened. But if she spurns you, I'll be proud to be your woman."

"Even though Gentry's the love of my life?"

"Yes. I'm not ashamed to admit I'd want you even if you're in love with another woman, provided you treat me and the girls with respect and affection. We could be a tidy little family, and together we can gradually rebuild this town. I don't mean to be bold, but I think you could do a lot worse than to have the girls and me by your side."

"It's your opinion Gentry still loves me?"

"Yes."

"But you don't think she'll come back with me?"

May bites her lip, then sighs. "It's not for me to say."

"I'm askin' for your honest opinion."

She pauses a moment, then says, "It depends on how she's been treated."

I feel my face, neck and ears burn.

"That makes sense," I say.

I ask to borrow a lantern. She gives me one, and I use it to light my way back to the *Spur*. I remember a time the streets glowed from the lamps and lanterns inside the build-in's and homes. It's a long, slow walk, and there ain't an ounce of joy in it.

CHAPTER 19

NEXT MORNIN' I finish my third drink of birch bark tea, while thinkin' about the two things that bothered me most of the night. When the women show up to haul more wood to the fire pit, I get May aside in the kitchen and ask, "Do you think it's possible the cattleman robbed the bank?"

She gives me an odd look. "No, Emmett. It was rebel soldiers. More than a dozen of them."

"What if the cattleman dressed up a dozen of his ranch hands in rebel uniforms and got them to rob the bank?"

May's look turns to sadness. "I know what you want me to say, Emmett, but I don't think that's what happened."

I nod. "Can I ask one more question?"

"Of course."

"Did this cattleman talk to anyone else in town?"

"I know Jim Bigsby met him, because his talk of Christmas trees in England had a big effect on Jim. He tried to get us to come into the saloon to see Gentry's tree, but..."

Her voice trails off, but her meanin's clear. She don't wish to insult me, but proper women don't frequent saloons where liquor and whores are offered to their husbands and sons.

"Did the cattleman talk to any other women?"

"Not that I know of."

"Thanks, May."

My body's feelin' stronger today, though my heart's got a hole in it. I found an old saw in Tom Collins's shed earlier this mornin' when I did an inventory of the wood left over from yesterday. I aim to saw the banister and spindles off the indoor stairs and use 'em for firewood. I ain't convinced Gentry's run off with this rich feller, but I ain't convinced she ain't, neither. I love Gentry, and I'm proud she's makin' sure our baby survives. But it don't sit well with me to think of her wigglin' between the sheets of another man's bed just 'cause he's got money. I know that sounds crazy, since from the age of twelve to the day I met her, Gentry whored day and night with men she didn't love, and did it just for the money. So why wouldn't she do it now, with a baby to support?

She would.

And I'd understand it.

It's just that I don't like it.

I agree with May about needin' to find Gentry to see if she still wants me. But I disagree with her thinkin' Gentry won't want me if the cattleman's treatin' her well. I believe she'll want me no matter how she's bein' treated, 'cause me and Gentry have somethin' special. And I believe Gentry feels the same way.

The women aren't as eager to help carry wood today after learnin' May gave me a shave and haircut at her place last night. They turned even frostier just now when I called May over for our little chat. But they're good-hearted women, and they'll do what they said they would.

Jim Bigsby's bustin' things left and right with his sledge hammer, and the women are haulin' the wood remnants to the fire pit. It takes six women to carry the wood cover I built for my jail hole, and they have to rest several times along the way. I marvel at these women, and how good-hearted and hard-workin' they are. I realize this is the only time most of them have ever stepped inside a saloon, and they ain't overjoyed about it, even though the place ain't been open for more'n a year. Of course, Jane and Claire came in here together the first mornin' after I became sheriff, to complain about problems they wanted me to fix. But they ain't been back from that day to this, to my knowledge.

Yesterday, all the tables and chairs were carted off to the fire pit, and all the interior doors 'cept the one that goes to my bedroom. They also hauled off the plywood Jim hammered over the front door to keep people out. Right now Jim's takin' the bar apart, and I'm makin' good progress sawin' the handrail and spindles off the steps. I hope things won't come down to me havin' to remove the steps, but after seein' how much we had to burn yesterday, and how little progress we made on the leg iron, I s'pect Tom Collins is right. I'll probably have to burn half the saloon to get these chains off my ankles.

It pains me to dismantle my home and business one plank at a time, just to build a fire. This is the place Gentry and me love. But I need proper use of my legs if I'm to find Gentry, since she could be anywhere. It's also possible I might have to rescue her. I'm more than ready to fight for her, but I'd have a hard time succeedin' against grown men with these chains on, since two days ago I couldn't even defend myself against two unarmed Indian boys sharin' a horse.

There's one woman in the bunch that keeps lookin' at me like she's tryin' to get my attention. She straggles behind when some of the others are liftin' a load, and when she hauls one off by herself, she rushes back sooner than the others. I'm terrible when it comes to readin' women's feelin's, but if I didn't know any better I'd think this partic'lar woman is more interested in me today than she was yesterday. And that surprises me, 'cause the woman showin' all this interest is Lilly Gee, the youngest, prettiest, available gal in town. Lilly's the one with the legendary behind that *didn't* walk over to speak to me yesterday. Accordin' to May, Lilly finds me too old and immoral to be a possible husband.

So it's likely I'm imaginin' the attention. She's probably just starin' at how different I appear without the whiskers and long hair. When she sees me lookin' at her, she immediately turns away, provin' she ain't interested.

So that's that.

But ten minutes later she walks toward me to fetch a load of spindles I've piled on the stair steps. She don't even look in my direction when pickin' them up, but whispers, "Emmett, I need to talk to you."

She gathers six spindles in her arms and walks past me while carryin' 'em. Though she don't speak, her eyes are locked on mine. I look around to see if anyone's watchin' us, and it might just be a coincidence, but every woman in the saloon is! I turn my back to Lilly, cover my mouth, and whisper, "Noon. Here."

She keeps walkin'.

CHAPTER 20

BY TEN O'CLOCK the women have stacked enough wood at Tom's fire pit to last a full day. I thank 'em, and they peel off one-by-one to go back to their houses and farms to do chores. By ten-thirty Jim's got the poker white-hot, and he starts in on my leg iron again, workin' that same spot we burned yesterday. Tom comes out to watch us awhile, but the heat chases him back inside. Now that Jim and I are alone, he says, "Nice haircut."

I look up and notice he's grinnin'.

He says, "Accordin' to Clara, May hasn't been with a man since the night she and Earl conceived the baby."

I shake my head, thinkin' how everyone always knows everyone else's business in Dodge. It's always been that way. Still, I wonder how May would feel if she knew her private business about Earl was known and discussed by everyone she knows. Because if Jim knows, everyone knows. I've always liked Jim's wife, Clara, and she's one of May's best friends, if not her very best friend. But apparently Clara ain't so good at keepin' secrets. Seein' Jim grinnin' at me makes me wonder if May told Clara what happened between her and me last night. That'd be awful embarrassin', 'specially if it ever got back to Gentry.

Jim appears to be expectin' a comment. Normally I wouldn't respond to such talk, but he's been workin' hard to help me, so I say "I wouldn't know about May and Earl, or what they did behind closed doors."

Jim don't let it end that easy. He says, "May's a comely woman. What is she, thirty-five?"

"Probably."

"If it's true she ain't been ridden' all these years, she'd probably have a lot of buckin' to do."

He winks at me.

I frown.

He removes the poker, and takes a cloth and wipes away the ash and shakes his head.

"We haven't made the first dent," he says.

"Let's try again," I say.

He stokes the fire and sets the tip of the poker in the flames and stands back from the heat. He wipes his brow with his shirt tail.

"Must be a million degrees," he says.

"Feels like it," I say. "Especially the circle around my ankle."

I dip some water onto my leg and let it run down so it can soak the cloth between my ankle and the leg iron. I've learned this is the best way to keep the cloth in place. Yesterday I dipped the water directly onto the cloth cuff and it moved the cloth and I had the dickens of a time tryin' to get it back where it needed to be. It were a painful lesson.

After ten minutes, Jim retrieves the poker and presses it against the burn spot that ain't made a dent yet. While he does that I think about how town gossip is a lot like leg irons. There's always someone stokin' the fire and pokin' at someone else, and the person gettin' poked has to go through a lot of pain. Gettin' others to stop talkin' about your business is probably as hard as gettin' shed of leg irons. And if they do stop talkin' about you, the feelin' of relief is probably similar to the relief I'll feel when I'm finally free from these cursed cuffs.

While he's pressin' the poker into the cuff, Jim says, "When I was eleven my parents bought a little farm outside Elwood, Illinois, that belonged to an older couple. They had a fishin' lake forty yards from the back porch that had been productive for twenty years."

I don't comment, figurin' if Jim has a point he'll get to it eventually. He presses the poker against the cuff some more, and says, "As they got older, the couple quit fishin' that hole, so the fish just kept growing and multiplying."

He looks at me.

"Can you imagine how much fun it was to dip my line in that fishin' hole after all those years it had been lyin' dormant?"

As a man who enjoys fishin' more than most, I start to chuckle. Then I stop, realizin' where his story's headin'. Before I have time to comment, he says, "May's got what I can only imagine is a glorious fishin' hole between her legs. And it's been dormant six years. I don't know about you, but I'd give a year of my life to be the first to dip my line into it."

I give him a look of disgust and say, "Well, why don't you then?"

He laughs. "I would, if it weren't for the fact she and Clara are best friends."

I don't know what to say, so I say nothin'.

After a few minutes of silence between us, Jim pulls the poker away and wipes the spot and says, "I'll be damned."

"What?"

"There's a dent!"

"What? Truly?"

"Feel for yourself."

I do. He's right, there's a dent. It's so small it's hardly worth mentionin'. But it's a dent, and that gives me hope.

I check the sun and decide it's gettin' close to noon.

"Let's take a break and hit it again around twelve-thirty," I say.

"I'd welcome that. I expect Clara's made enough lunch for both of us," he says, "if you'd care to join us."

"Thanks, but no. I'll want to feed and water Rudy and Scarlett."

"Need some help with the pump?"

"The womenfolk were kind enough to fill my bucket this mornin'."

He gives me a look like he's about to say somethin' smart about that, but sees the look on my face and decides against it. He fusses with the fire a minute, movin' the un-burned wood away from the flames. When the flame dies down he says, "See you in an hour," and heads home. I stay put, waitin' for my cuff to cool. If I try to stand up now, it'll shift and burn a hole in my skin. So I sit and watch the embers glow, and think about Jim, and what he'd said.

I'd never known my friend to talk so much about forni-catin' before, but of course, durin' the years I knew Jim he was pokin' our house whores regularly, so he probably didn't have much reason to openly reflect on May's fishin' hole, nor how long it had been lyin' dormant. After thinkin' about that for awhile, I turn my thoughts to Lilly Gee, and wonder what she wants to talk about. I think about how hard her life's been, bein' so young and livin' years with a man who's brain dead to the extent he sits around and hoots like an owl all day. I wonder how he died, and that reminds me how my Aunt Booger once told me half the men in the county died after bein' poisoned by their wives. I was fifteen when she said that. I didn't believe it then, and don't believe it still. But it does make me think.

After my cuff cools, I get to my feet and shuffle down the street, turn the corner, and walk into the front door of the *Spur*. Lilly ain't here yet, so I take the animals outside and let 'em do their business. Then I give 'em some water, and a couple of corn dodgers. I help myself to some of the cracklins and remind myself how much I owe the owner of this fine horse, Scarlett.

When I bring the animals back inside, Lilly Gee's standin' in the kitchen.

CHAPTER 21

I AIN'T LOOKIN' for a woman to replace Gentry. But if I were, this is where I'd start. Lilly Gee is tall and slender, with long, reddish-blond hair that's always fresh-combed, and eyes the color of a ripe persimmon. Her skin is clear of any type of blemish. Her teeth are bright white and perfectly straight, which is quite rare, in my experience. I can't speak to her smile, for I've never seen her wear one. Then again, our paths have only crossed a few times. I've passed her in the street, waited behind her in line at the saddle store once, saw her at the general store a time or two. On each of these occasions she spoke only the slightest, or not at all.

"Thank you for seeing me," she says.

"Do you have news of Gentry?"

She gives me a confused look. Then says, "If that's why you agreed to see me, I'm afraid I owe you an apology."

"No, don't be silly. It's just that you didn't speak to me yesterday, so I figured maybe you remembered somethin' afterward. Somethin' about Gentry."

She looks around. "There's no place to sit."

"I'm sorry about that."

She looks at the chains around my ankles.

"Will you get them off?"

"I will. But it's gonna take time."

"I'm sorry."

"You been through worse."

Her eyes grow moist. She turns away and walks to the corner of the room, past the counter that's mostly on the floor in pieces. She finds a small part of it that ain't been smashed by Jim's sledge hammer yet, and backs up against it. I think about steppin' closer to her, but decide she probably went there to put more space between us. Then I look behind me and see Rudy starin' at us.

"He won't hurt you," I say.

"I'm not comfortable around bears."

I walk over to Rudy and lead him away from the door. He plops down in his old corner. "Scarlett?" I say. The horse's ears perk up. "Come."

Scarlett walks over. "Stay with Rudy," I say.

Scarlett turns away and walks back where she was before I called her over, which puts a frown on my face. Sometimes she's brilliant, smarter than a human. Other times, she's definitely a horse, and a mule-headed one at that. I go back in the kitchen and say, "Sorry about that." I wait a few seconds

onds for her to speak. She don't, so I say, "What did you want to talk about?"

She lowers her eyes. Her lips tremble. "There's a man," she says.

I wait for her to say more.

She looks at me with pleadin' eyes.

I say, "Tell me about him."

Then she blurts out somethin' that makes my blood run cold. "He's a cattleman," she says. "From England."

I wait for her to get up her courage, but she's got herself upset, and begins to cry. I don't know if I should walk over and try to comfort her, or wait it out. Last time a woman cried at me I wound up naked under her kitchen table. Since I ain't got a kitchen table, I decide to wait it out. After a few minutes she says, "I'm sorry. I know you've got your own troubles."

"Please," I say. "Tell me about this man, and why he's got you so upset."

She shrugs and looks away.

"Start by tellin' me his name."

She looks around, as if someone might be listenin'. I say, "You can speak freely. We're alone."

"David Wilson."

"And he's a cattleman from England?"

She nods.

"And what's David Wilson done to get you in such a state?"

"He won't leave me alone."

"Is he in town now?"

"No sir. I don't think so."

"But he's been here several times?"

She nods.

"Has he hurt you in any way?"

She shakes her head no.

"But?"

"But he won't leave me alone."

"Tell me what he's doin'."

"He keeps showing up at my house."

"How often?"

"Sometimes two days in a row. Sometimes at night. Sometimes he doesn't show up for a month. Then he comes back."

"And what's he say?"

"He wants me to run off with him. Wants me to marry him, and have his children. Says he's very wealthy and he'll take care of me."

"Do you believe him?"

"Doesn't matter what I believe. I'm not interested. But he won't take no for an answer."

"When did all this start?"

"About six months ago."

That's about the time both Jim and May said Gentry left. But May believes Gentry left with David Wilson. I want to ask Lilly if Wilson ever mentioned Gentry, but I'm pretty sure she'll say no, and worse, she'll think I don't care about what Wilson is doin' to her. And I do, because her story and Gentry's are close enough to be twins.

"Is David Wilson threatenin' you?"

"Yes."

"How?"

She looks around again. "He said if I tell anyone he's been coming around, he'll kill the person I tell."

"He'll kill them himself? Or have someone else do it?"

"He didn't say."

"But you believe him?"

"Yes."

"So I'm the first person you've told?"

"Yes."

"Why tell me today, and not yesterday?"

She turns her head away, like she's embarrassed.

"It's okay. You can say it. No matter how it sounds."

"When I heard you were in town I was excited. I mean, you used to be the sheriff and all. I couldn't wait to tell you. But when I saw you..."

"What?"

"You seemed so old and helpless. I didn't think you'd be able to help me."

"And now?"

"I guess you've eaten a nice meal, got your hair and beard cut. You're moving around better. Today you seem more like a sheriff and less like a dying man. No offense."

"That's alright," I say. Then add, "When Mr. Wilson shows up, is he alone?"

"Yes, but two men are always standing guard. If he's at my place, the two men can always be seen on top of the hills facing my house."

"Gunmen?"

"I think so. I've never seen them up close. But probably."

"Does Wilson appear to be a violent man?"

"He's never thrown a fit, or tried to force me to do anything. But he told me he's losing his patience. He said he always gets what he wants, one way or the other, and he's decided I'm to be his wife. Said the next time he comes to town, he aims to snatch me up. He said I'd grow to love him, over time."

"That sounds violent to me," I say.

"Me too."

"Do you keep a gun?"

"Yes sir, but I don't have any bullets for it. Nor could I shoot a man."

"Even if he was trying to steal you away?"

She thinks about it briefly, then says, "I could never shoot a man."

I nod. "Where's his ranch?"

"Somewhere in Texas."

"He won't say where?"

"No sir, though I've asked."

"Couldn't be too far into Texas," I say. "Else he wouldn't be able to come so often."

Lilly doesn't say anythin' to that, so I ask, "How long since his last visit?"

"About a week."

"Did he say when he'd be back?"

"No sir. Just said when he comes I better be ready to say yes."

I pause a minute before sayin', "Lilly, your house is a half mile from town. Long as you're stayin' there, I can't protect you. But if you'll stay in one of the rooms upstairs, I can make sure nothin' bad happens to you."

"That wouldn't be proper."

"It wouldn't be proper for Wilson to snatch you up and take you away from your home, neither."

"I can't stay here. People will talk."

"They'll talk worse if Wilson steals you."

She starts to cry again, but softly. She dabs her eyes with a handkerchief I'd swear she didn't possess a minute ago. What is it with Dodge women and their handkerchiefs?

"Would you stay with Jim and Clara?"

"It wouldn't be right to drag them into this. I do believe he'd kill them."

I frown. "Then you got no choice. You need to move in here. If you want, I'll see if I can talk one of the women into stayin' here with you."

"Who would do that?"

"I believe Margaret Stallings might."

She thinks about it. Then says, "If Margaret will stay in the same room with me, I will take you up on your kind offer. But what about Mr. Wilson?"

"When he shows up in town I'll kill him."

"What if he brings several men with him?"

"I'll kill them all. You've got my word."

"What if you get the leg irons off before he shows up? Won't you be ridin' off to find Gentry?"

"Yes, but that might be quite a long while. Surely David Wilson will show up before then."

She nods. "I have a feeling he'll be back within the week."

"There you go," I say. I realize I'm starin', and she notices it, but I can't help it. Her handkerchief is gone. But where?

Lilly says, "Will you talk to Margaret, or should I?"

"I'll ask her."

She pauses. Somethin's on her mind.

"What?"

"What about the bear?"

"Rudy? I'll put him in my room."

"Um...there's no doors except for the one in your room."

She's right. I'd forgot that part.

"You and Margaret can bunk in my room. Me and Rudy will sleep in one of the others."

"Thank you, Emmett."

"You're quite welcome."

She walks over to me and gives me a quick hug. She's tall enough that her forehead touches my cheek. I smell a scent on her that ain't perfume or soap, but sweet just the same. It's a natural scent, and a nice one. This is a fine figure of a woman. Not in Gentry's league, but mighty close. She suddenly surprises me by kissin' my cheek. I turn my face toward hers, but she backs up quickly, so I won't get the wrong impression. I think about how I've been kissed by two proper women in the space of sixteen hours, which ain't somethin' most men can say.

As Lilly walks away my eyes are drawn to the gentle sway of her hips. She has that same mesmerizin' way of walkin' Gentry has, but Lilly's is natural, while Gentry's is practiced. That don't mean one walks better than the other, 'cause both would cause a man to stare.

I shake away such thoughts of Lilly and Gentry's behinds, and replace them with the thought that Gentry didn't run off with Wilson! If she had, he wouldn't be makin' matrimonial offers to Lilly. The fact he never called on Lilly till Gentry disappeared tells me Gentry got away, and he was forced to find someone else.

I figure Gentry found a way to hide Rudy and get away from David Wilson. And if that happened, my best friend, Shrug, must've had a hand in it.

I say a silent thank you to Shrug, wherever he may be. And expect wherever he is, he's guardin' Gentry and Scarlett Rose.

I'm more convinced than ever that all three of 'em are in Springfield at Rose's ranch.

When I shuffle out the front door, I see May standin' there, waitin' for me.

I smile.

Why, howdy May!" I say, enthusiastically.

She walks two steps toward me and slaps my face hard. Before I can ask why she done that, she turns and stomps off.

CHAPTER 22

IT'S TOO EARLY for Jim to be back from lunch, so I head down the narrow dirt road called Front Street, toward the second-to-last house on the west edge of town. As I approach, Margaret comes out the front door and starts walkin' toward me.

"I saw you kickin' up dust a block away," she says. "Were you looking for me?"

"I was."

"Why?"

"I've got a big favor to ask."

"I hope you don't want me to pull your pecker like May Gray did last night."

I start to say somethin', then don't, but feel my face turnin' red. After awhile I say, "She told you that?"

"There aren't many secrets in this town, Emmett. Not with ten women tryin' to win the heart of a lovesick bachelor."

"In any case, that ain't the favor."

"Good. Because I'd have to decline."

I take a deep breath, then let it out slowly.

She says, "Where'd you get the horse?"

"Excuse me?"

She points behind me. I turn to look, and nearly come out of my skin. There's a gorgeous roan-colored stallion standin' four feet behind me. I didn't hear him sneak up on me, which means it simply couldn't have happened.

"You saw him walkin' toward me?"

"Of course. Why?"

"I didn't hear him come up on me."

"So?"

"I've got the finest ears of anyone I know, 'cept for two friends of mine who ain't normal."

"Your hearing is that good?"

"Ma'am, I can hear a turtle peein' in a lake, underwater!"

"Well, I heard him, so what does that say about me?"

I shake my head.

"What's wrong?" she says.

"This just don't make sense."

Like Scarlett, this horse has two saddlebags, and appears to be waitin' for me. I briefly wonder if maybe this horse only rides east. If so, maybe he can take me part way to Springfield, which is south-east of Dodge.

"He ain't mine," I say.

"He acts like he is," Margaret says.

"I've never seen him before. Have you?"

"No."

I move a few steps to the side, so I can keep an eye on both Margaret and the horse at the same time. It don't pay to turn my back to a horse I don't know, nor a town woman who can hear better than me. I wonder if she's about to suddenly sport a handkerchief in her hand. I almost feel like kickin' up dust to see if I can determine where the damn things are comin' from. If I could draw my gun as fast as these town women draw their handkerchiefs, I'd feel a lot more comfortable goin' up against David Wilson and his hired guns. Which reminds me why I came to see Margaret in the first place.

On the trail men get to the point quick. In town, you're supposed to be polite, and wait for what Gentry calls an "ebb in the conversation" before speakin'. I notice the conversation between Margaret and me has died down like the flames in Tom's fire pit, so I take the opportunity to tell Margaret all the things Lilly Gee told me at the *Spur* a few minutes ago, and ask if she'd be willin' to stay there with Lilly and me till David Wilson comes back to town. I ask if she can come over around six tonight.

"I don't want to upset May," she says.

"May just slapped my face!"

"She—what did you do?"

"I don't know. First, I was talkin' to Lilly. Then I came out the door and May slapped my face, hard."

"Did Lilly come out first?"

"She did."

Margaret chuckles.

"What?"

"Can you really be so naïve when it comes to women?"

"It appears I can. What happened?"

She clucks some more and laughs, and says, "Oh, Emmett!"

After she's done doin' that for awhile she says, "Well, I'll ask May. If it's all right with her, I'll stay with Lilly a few days."

"Why would you need to ask May?"

"She might be jealous."

"Why?"

"She might read something wrong in you coming to me for help, instead of her."

"She's got three kids to keep up with at her own place."

Margaret shakes her head. But smiles.

"What?"

"Your actions are completely logical, but May won't see it that way."

I sigh, remove my hat, run my hand through my hair, put my hat back on. "How will May see it?"

"Like I was your first choice, then she pulled your pecker, and you still invited Lilly, her biggest rival, into your saloon. Then you invited me. May thinks you've got a thing for me."

"I'd rather you didn't speak to May about it."

"Why not?"

"David Wilson said he'd kill anyone that finds out about him visitin' Lilly."

"And yet you told me."

"That don't sound good on me, does it? Truth is I figured I could protect you if you're at the *Spur*."

We stand there in the street a minute quietly in a sort of triangle. Margaret, me, and the new horse.

"You should check the saddlebags," Margaret says.

"This ain't my horse. A man could get shot goin' through another man's things."

"Could a woman get shot for looking?"

While I'm thinkin' of a respectful way to say "hell yes!" Margaret walks up to the horse and opens one of the bags.

"Hmm," she says. "That's something I've never seen in a cowboy's saddlebag."

"What?"

She pulls out a thick bar of lye soap.

I frown. "What in *tarnation*—"

Margaret cocks her head at me. "I take it you don't approve of keeping clean on the trail."

"You could clean an army with that much soap. Is there nothin' else in that bag?"

She steps on tiptoes and peers in.

"Nope. Just the soap."

"That seems like a complete waste of space."

"How long since you've had a bath, cowboy?" Margaret says.

She has a way with words that ain't half as blunt as May's, but I notice they both get to the same point, which is to make me feel like I should've been doin' somethin' all along that hadn't bothered me till they spoke about it.

"Now that you mention it, I ain't had a soap bath since I got captured."

"Never look a gift horse in the mouth," she says, smilin'.

She puts the soap back in the saddlebag and moves around the stallion in a wide half-circle, like you'd want to do with any horse you don't know too well. I watch her face as she peers into the second saddlebag. She looks back at me, then into the bag again, and I notice she's wearin' a puzzled look.

"What?" I say.

But Margaret don't respond. Instead, she walks back to where I'm standin' in the dirt road.

"What's the matter?" I say, but Margaret's too busy to answer. She shocks me by gettin' down on one knee like she's about to propose. I look around, embarrassed. If May sees her proposin' to me I might get worse than slapped.

I might get shot!

But Margaret don't propose marriage. Instead, she pulls up my right pant leg and touches the lock on my leg iron.

"Hold still," she says.

Now she's reachin' up in the key hole with her fingers.

"It can't be tripped," I say. "I've tried a thousand times with twigs and rocks and bits of wire. Nothin' works."

She pulls up the other pant leg and does the same with that one.

"This is your horse, Emmett."

"It ain't my dang horse, Margaret. I never laid eyes on it till just now."

As if Margaret ain't shocked me enough today by knowin' what happened with May, and hearin' the horse when I didn't, and gettin' down on one knee in the middle of the street, she does somethin' that shocks me more than all the rest put together.

She stands and kisses me flush on the mouth!

CHAPTER 23

I AIN'T BEEN kissed this much since the night of the big storm in Edna, Oklahoma, when I was the only man in town who thought to take shelter in the local whore house. But them weren't proper women, so I s'pect the record I'm settin' here in Dodge City's the one to beat.

Before I get too prideful about it, I need to think up a sensible explanation to give Gentry about all that's happened between me and these town women. Especially May. Should I tell it the way it happened? I run through it in my mind. Why did I go to May's house? To find out what she knew about Gentry. Then what happened? I ate dinner. Then May gave me a shave and haircut. Then May got naked and came at me like a cyclone. By the end of the evenin', I'm naked, hidin' under her kitchen table. As I think on it in my head, Gentry might wonder why I waited so short to get naked, and so long to find out what May knew about Gentry's whereabouts.

Margaret seems to know women better than most. I'll ask her how I should tell it to Gentry. But this don't seem to be the time to ask Margaret, because she just kissed me. It was just once, and quick, and now a second time, like she means it. Then she backs up and pulls the saddlebags from the horse, and starts walkin' toward her house.

"Follow me!" she says.

I shuffle behind her, wonderin' what she's got in mind. She already said she wouldn't pull my pecker, so that appears to be off the table.

Margaret don't have a parlor like May. When you walk in her front door there's a kitchen on the left and a sleepin' area on the right. I notice everythin's tidy and clean.

She points to the bed.

"Sit," she says.

I do.

"Now lift up your pants."

"What have you got in mind?" I say.

She looks at me and laughs. Then pulls a large key from one of the saddlebags. I recognize it as the type of key the soldiers used to lock my leg irons. I come up off the bed and stand.

"Sit back down," she says. "I reckon you won't be able to do this on your own."

Just as quickly as I'd got excited, I'm already dragged down in disappointment.

"That's a new key. It won't turn these old locks."

"Just sit down," she says.

I sit back down on the side of the bed, and she sits on the floor in front of me, and places the key in the lock. To my surprise, it fits. She turns it, and I hear a click. Just one little click, and tears suddenly flood my eyes.

"Oh, *Emmett!*" she says. "Oh, my *word!*"

She pulls the leg iron open and off, and my eyes roll up into my head.

I reach out to her and she rises to her knees and hugs me back. We're swayin' back and forth, holdin' the hug. My tears of joy wet the hair on top of her head. After awhile we settle back down so Margaret can unlock the second lock.

But the second lock won't open.

She tries it several times, then frowns, removes the key, and puts her fingers in the keyhole again.

"This one's too rusted," she says.

"Well, I won't be ungrateful. You saved me days, maybe weeks, of pain."

She sits there, starin' at the cuff.

"On the bright side," I say, "I'm not just shed of the cuff, but half the chain as well. So my left leg can finally heal while we work on the right one."

Margaret's deep in thought. She puts her fingers inside the lock yet again, works them around. When she removes them, she gives them a close inspection. Then she looks at me and smiles.

"What's it worth to you?" she says.

"What do you mean?"

"What would you give to get this leg iron off?"

Her question throws me.

"Can you get it off?"

"I can."

"Seriously?"

She nods.

"What do you want?"

"Somethin' you can't give just yet. But I'll accept your promise about it."

I know what she wants. She wants me to promise if things don't work out with Gentry, I'll pick her instead of May. It's a bold thing for her to do, trade my freedom for a promise to break another woman's heart. A woman who'd keep me from bein' free would surely withhold her feminine charms from her husband. Assumin' we ever got married. But if she's so mean-spirited as to expect such a promise, I aim to make her say it out loud.

"You can really set me free?"

"I really can."

"What do I have to promise?"

"You want me to say it out loud?"

"Yes."

"If you find Gentry and wind up coming back to Dodge..."

"Yes?"

"I want to be mayor."

"You *what?*"

"I want to be mayor."

"Why, you can be mayor right now!"

"Not without a sheriff to enforce my rules."

I think on what type of town Margaret might run.

"Would you be against drinkin'?"

"Of course not! Drinking attracts men."

"Whorin'?"

"Same thing."

"Fightin'? Cussin'?"

"Your job is to control the fighting. And I could care less about the cussing, provided it's not directed at the innocent."

I'm confused.

"Then what's the point of bein' mayor?"

I want to establish a county school. And a playground. And a town hall, where couples can dance on Friday nights and come together for town socials."

"Why, them are *fine* ideas!"

"Thank you."

"I just can't imagine you'd withhold my freedom for that kind of promise."

Margaret gets to her feet while sayin', "How many towns have you been to in your life, Emmett?"

"I don't know. Too many to count."

"How many of those towns had women mayors?"

"Well...not many."

"Any?"

"Not that I can recall."

"If this town ever starts to grow again, and you go back to bein' sheriff, you're going to face a lot of opposition to having a female mayor."

"I reckon that's true."

"I'll release you from your chains, but I aim to hold you to your promise."

"Margaret?"

"Yes?"

"Your ideas are so good I'll give you my promise even if you can't get the leg iron off."

She smiles.

"Thanks, Emmett. You're an unusually open-minded man."

She pulls the lye soap from the other saddlebag and flashes a wide grin.

"Do you aim to give me a bath?" I say.

"Would you like me to?"

CHAPTER 24

I NEVER HEARD of soapin' a lock before, but Margaret's older and wiser than me, and thank goodness she's the one I was standin' with when the horse showed up, because my chains are finally off. Like Scarlett, the roan stallion follows me step by step all the way to Lilly Gee's house.

"Your chains are gone," she says.

I nod.

"Then I suppose you've come to tell me you're leaving town?"

"I'm itchin' to find Gentry, but I'll stay awhile and see what happens. Maybe Wilson will show."

"And if he doesn't?"

"We'll cross that bridge when we come to it."

"Have you spoken to Margaret?"

"I have, and she's agreed to bunk with you."

"What time should I come tonight?" she says.

"Around six ought to work."

She thinks about it a minute, then says, "Thank you, Emmett. That's real kind of you. I'll be on time."

I tip my hat, and head back to the *Spur*. I walk the stallion in carefully, 'cause Rudy's inside, and most horses shy away from bears. To my amazement, neither the stallion, Scarlett, nor Rudy seem bothered by the other. When I'm sure they're comfortable bein' in the same room together, I head to Tom Collins's fire pit, where I know Jim will be waitin'.

As I approach, I see he's got the fire roarin'.

"Have you told May yet?" he says.

"May?"

"Have you told her?"

"About what?"

"Why, Margaret, of course!"

"What about her?"

"Heard she offered you a new horse as a dowry, then got down on one knee and proposed to you right in the middle of town. You said yes, and she kissed you so hard she dragged you to her house and gave you a sound fucking."

"*What?* You heard all that?"

"I did."

"Well it ain't true."

He frowns. "Which part?"

"First off, we weren't in the middle of town. We were out on Front Street, not twenty yards from her place."

Jim takes off his hat, places it over his heart. "I can't even imagine how long her field has remained unplowed. Did she cry?"

"Cry?"

"You know, tears of gratitude."

"No she didn't cry!"

"Personally, I'd have picked Lilly. I hear she's a good kisser. Is that true?"

I sigh. "Have you even noticed I'm shed of my leg irons?"

He hadn't. He looks at my ankles.

"How the hell...?"

"You wouldn't believe me if I told you."

Jim looks at the wood stacked around the fire pit.

"Guess we ought to salvage what we can and take it back to your place," he says.

CHAPTER 25

MY PAIN IS half what it was last night, so either the birch bark tea is workin', or maybe I'm just so happy to be out of my chains I don't notice it so much.

I've got a decision to make.

Less than two hours ago I invited Lilly Gee and Margaret Stallings to stay at the *Spur* till David Wilson shows up. At that time I was deep in my chains and figured I'd be stuck in Dodge at least two weeks, maybe more. If one of these horses will take me southwest, I could be at Rose's ranch in four days. And if they *won't* ride me there, I can *walk* to her place in ten days.

I have no desire to stay in Dodge to wait for that scum-suckin' David Wilson. Hell, he might decide not to show up for a *month*! Thinkin' thoughts of not bein' with Gentry for a whole month, while knowin' I'm only 400 miles away, is pure agony. I could ask Jim to stay at the *Spur* and keep an eye on Lilly and Margaret till I get back with Gentry, and no one would blame me.

Except that Jim ain't a shooter.

If Wilson *does* happen to show up with his men, the result will be hard to live with.

I sigh.

The only right thing to do is stay here and protect Lilly Gee. I was sheriff of Dodge when I got captured, and reckon I'm sheriff, still.

I spend the rest of the afternoon haulin' what wood I can carry to the *Spur* with my sore ribs and back. Jim is carryin' three times my load without complaint, and I'm beholdin' to him. Otherwise, I wouldn't allow him to make the comments he does.

"How would a man choose between Gentry and Lilly?" he says, as we work. "On the one hand, Gentry's prettier. On the other, Lilly's a proper woman, and ain't been with but one man, so her time 'tween the sheets is more special. On the one hand, Gentry's a whore, so her time 'tween the sheets is the best money can buy. On the other hand, Lilly'd be a great mother. On the other hand, Gentry'd be a great wife. On the—wait. How many hands is that?"

"You're up to five hands already, and ain't said a damn thing. They're different women, and it don't matter which a man would choose, 'cause I already made my choice, and so did you."

"True," Jim says, "but here's the question I always wondered."

"What's that?" I say, bein' cordial to a vulgar man who's doin' the work of three in this God-awful heat.

Jim says, "Do you think during these last years Lilly's husband was able to give her a steady poking?"

I frown and decide not to comment for fear I'll lose my temper. But no sooner had I not spoken than Jim says, "Which one would you rather fuck after a long, dormant spell: a young filly like Lilly, or a seasoned mare like May?"

"This type a' talk don't interest me," I say, with an even-tempered voice. "Nor does it help you."

"Well," he says, "On the one hand, Lilly ain't got the experience to properly please a man. On the other, her skin is tight, and milky-white, and—"

And it goes on like that all afternoon, till we haul the last load of wood back to the *Spur*. While we're stackin' it in the center of the saloon, Margaret shows up with her carpet-bag and Jim says, "Whoa, what's this?"

"Margaret's stayin' here a few days with me and Lilly."

"She's *what?*"

"I'm surprised you don't already have an opinion on it."

Jim grins. "I reckon I'll form one soon as May finds out."

CHAPTER 26

SIX TURNS INTO seven, and Jim comes back with a bottle of rye that's got maybe two shots left in it.

Lilly ain't showed up yet, so I sit and have a pull with him. Margaret's in the kitchen, fryin' pork fat for the green beans she brought from her garden.

"Where did Gentry put the Christmas tree?" I ask.

Jim points to the open area left of the bar.

"The quiet corner," I say.

There used to be a table and chairs there, where I'd conduct my sheriffin' business.

"Tell me what you know about the cattleman from England who told Gentry about Christmas trees."

Jim scrunches up his face and squints, tryin' to conjure up a memory.

"There's not much to tell," he says. "Man's name is David Wilkins, and he's got a ranch somewhere southwest of here."

"He's rich?"

"Claims to be."

"Did he ever come back that you know of?"

"Once or twice, on his way to or from St. Joe."

"Do you—"

I pause.

"What?" Jim asks.

I'm thinkin' back on the conversation. Somethin' ain't right.

"You're lost in thought, Emmett," Jim says.

I bite the bottom of my lip. Then say, "Wilson."

"Huh?"

"The cattleman's name. It's Wilson, not Wilkins."

He thinks a minute. "No, it's Wilkins."

"You sure?"

"Ought to be. I've sat and drunk with him twice."

"Maybe you misunderstood his name. After drinkin', it's easy to mistake a man's last name."

"That's true, but I wouldn't forget Wilkins. It's my mother's maiden name."

I think about that as I bid Jim goodbye and tell Margaret I'm headin' to Lilly's to fetch her back.

She pulls the skillet off the fire.

"I'll come with you," she says.

"No, go ahead and finish your cookin'. We'll be back by the time you're finished."

I grab the rifle from the scabbard that was attached to Scarlett that first day, and check to see how many bullets it has, hopin' whoever owns the horse and all these corn dodgers and pork skins will allow me to pay him back some day for usin' 'em.

I notice Margaret seems uneasy.

"What's wrong?"

"You're leaving me here alone? Cooking food? With a bear in the house?"

"Good point. I'll give him a corn dodger, and leave some for you to give him, case he starts annoyin' you. You'll be safe."

"You're sure about that?"

"Absolutely. Rudy would never hurt you. Even if he were starvin'."

Margaret's comforted, but not comfortable. She warily puts the skillet back on the fire and pushes the pork around to coat the bottom. Then she puts the beans in the pan and starts movin' 'em around. Adds a little water to it, I assume, since I hear a loud sizzle as I head out the front door.

These August nights in Kansas don't get dark till nearly nine, so there's plenty of light as I head toward Lilly's. I could try to ride one of the horses, but don't trust 'em not to throw me if I want to make a turn they don't approve of. It's all right. I'm so pleased to have full use of my legs, I'm happy to enjoy the act of walkin' without pain for the first time in twenty-eight months.

Though Lilly's house is only a half-mile from town, it's secluded, and there are grassy knolls on two sides high enough to block the view of every part of the structure 'cept the roof. The first knoll comes into view a quarter mile from her place. What I'm thinkin' is Lilly was frightened about bein' kidnapped by David Wilson, or Wilkins, or whatever his name is. I'm also thinkin' she's almost two hours late. I'm also thinkin' she told me when the man came callin' in the past he had two men standin' guard who might be gunmen. If they *are*, and if they're *here*, I could get shot long before reachin' her front door.

Because I'm thinkin' all these thoughts, I stop and look carefully at the knoll.

And see no one.

That's a good sign, but Lilly's still almost two hours late.

I get off the trail and duck into the tall grass and slowly make my way to the back of the first knoll.

And still see no one.

On my belly now, on top of the knoll, I part the grass enough to where I can see the front of Lilly's house. Right away I can tell somethin's not right. If you were afraid three men were after you, would you leave your front door slightly open?

Of course not.

And neither would Lilly.

But her front door *is* slightly open. I think about calling out her name, but that could backfire on me, since I don't know who might be in there. I turn my body a few feet to the right and part a little of that grass, hopin' to see if any horses are tied to the railin' in front of the barn.

But there ain't no horses.

I crawl on my belly all the way down the knoll and work my way very slowly and quietly up the second knoll, and see someone twenty yards in front of me on the ground, aimin' a rifle at the front door.

It's Lilly.

I stand up slowly and clear my throat. She gasps and spins around and I fire a bullet right between her beautiful, persimmon-colored eyes.

CHAPTER 27

I'M NOT SURE why Lilly wanted to ambush me, but after shootin' her I crouch down in case anyone's inside the house. I give ample time for someone to come out with guns blazin', but remember I didn't see or hear any horses just now when I shot, and usually you'd expect to hear somethin' from a horse when a gun's fired nearby. I wait a few minutes, then walk down the hill to the house. When I get there, I push the front door hard. It squeaks on its hinges somethin' fierce, hits the wall behind it with force. When I hear the sound of wood on wood I know there's no one hidin' behind it.

I enter the room, and glance around at her furnishin's. Lilly's house only has the one big room and two small bedrooms. Both bedroom doors are open, and the rooms are small enough that I could see if someone was hidin' in 'em, 'less they're hidin' under the bed. I peek under both beds and see nothin'.

In the bedroom Lilly uses, there's a closet.

The door is closed.

I knock on it, then say, "I'm fixin' to shoot through the door, so if someone's in there, you better call out now or suffer the consequences."

Then I listen. If someone's in there I expect they'll cry out or scamper away from the door. Either way I'll hear 'em. But there's no sound, so I push that door open and brace myself against the unknown, same way I did thirty years ago, when I opened the bedroom door and found my ma and pa killed by Indians.

But there are no Indians in the closet, and no dead people, neither.

I turn to leave, but somethin' on Lilly's nightstand catches my eye.

Her Bible.

A woman's bible is the best source of information there is. Inside are all the names, dates, and special occasions of her life. People will lie to their friends and family members about everythin', but they never lie to their Bible. It's their heritage, and lineage, and as I open it and scan the family tree I quickly find the reason Lilly set me up to shoot me tonight.

Her maiden name.

Hartman.

I knew Sam Hartman had kinfolk all through Kansas, but had no reason to suspect he was related to Lilly Gee.

With all the gossip that goes on in small towns, there are few secrets, to be sure. But somehow, Lilly managed to keep this one. Far as any of us knew, her maiden name was Parker.

I've said it a thousand times. The biggest reason I hate killin' people is their relatives. It just don't sit well with a father when I kill his son, or a boy when I kill his pa, or a girl like Lilly, when I killed her brother, Sam, twenty-eight months ago.

What don't sit well with me is I now realize all bets are off as far as what might've happened to Gentry. Since Wilkins has *not* been botherin' Lilly, it's likely he either kidnapped Gentry, or talked her into runnin' off with him. It's just as likely his ranch ain't in Texas, since I've only got Lilly's word on that.

Lilly obviously heard the story about Gentry and Wilkins. She got the last name wrong, but was smart enough to use the same story to lure me out to her house tonight. She rightly assumed I'd come to fetch her if she didn't show up at the *Spur* on time. I'd come here, call out her name, get no answer. I'd walk a little closer, see the door slightly open, walk up to it slowly, and she'd put a bullet in my head.

That's why Lilly didn't approach me when she was in line with the other women yesterday. She hated me for killin' her brother, and came up with a plan to tell me Wilkins threatened to kidnap her.

Which means Lilly spoke to someone about Wilkins and Gentry, someone she knew would tell me about him last night.

May Gray.

CHAPTER 28

IT'S DUSKY WHEN I knock on May's door. Instead of bein' angry with me, she seems happily surprised.

"Howdy, Emmett," she says.

"Hi."

"Would you like to come in?"

"I'd rather you come out on the porch and close the door so the girls won't hear."

She's wearin' an amused expression on her face, but says, "Very well, then."

She comes outside. Says, "I'm sorry I slapped you."

"That's all right."

"Do you know why I was angry?"

"No ma'am."

"Do you want me to try to explain?"

"Maybe some other time."

She nods, then says, "I heard you proposed to Margaret."

"That ain't true."

She laughs. "I never believed it. You're Gentry's man, through and through. And you'll be Gentry's man long after she's moved on."

She gives me a moment to agree or deny. When I don't, she says, "What did you want to discuss?"

I study May's face while sayin', "Lilly knew about Gentry and the cattleman."

Several strange looks come over her face. Like she's worried, then curious, then puzzled. Finally, she speaks. "I might've mentioned something to Lilly as a precautionary tale."

"What's that mean?"

Lilly's young and beautiful, like Gentry. I was concerned the cattleman might come after her, too."

"But you don't remember his name?"

"No. As I said last night, Gentry never disclosed it."

"That's odd."

"How so?"

"Lilly knew his name."

"The cattleman?"

I nod. "Know what I think?"

"Tell me."

"I think Gentry ran into Lilly that night she was upset, not you. And told Lilly about this cattleman. And since this town thrives on gossip and rumor, somewhere along the line, probably yesterday mornin', Lilly told you about the cattleman and Gentry. She said you could make it seem like it happened to you, since she wasn't interested in me."

There's a long silence between us while May's face grows beet red. "You're calling me a liar?"

"Yes, ma'am."

She slaps me again, full force. Then says, "Do you have anything else to say to me?"

"I do. Lilly's dead."

"*What?*"

"I killed her, not thirty minutes ago. At her place."

CHAPTER 29

"I'M SORRY I'VE got no chairs and tables," I say, sippin' a cup of birch bark tea, "but I'll be brief. The reason I called this emergency meetin' is to inform you I'm still sheriff of Dodge City. And in that..."

I look over at Margaret, who says, "Capacity."

"Capacity?"

She nods.

"In that capacity, of bein' town sheriff and all, I shot and killed someone tonight."

Everyone starts murmerin' till Tom Collins asks, "Is it someone we know?"

It's hard to decide who's in worse shape: George Reed, who's dyin' of lead poisonin', or Tom Collins, our one-armed, one-legged former blacksmith. George's body is completely gray, while Tom's is yellow with black spots. It's also hard to tell who stinks the most. Yesterday George would a' won hands down. But Tom took a turn for the worse and smells like fresh entrails. I think about it a minute and decide it's close, but George wins the stink contest by a nose.

By tomorrow it'll change. Though neither man looks likely to survive the night, I give 'em credit for their public display of civic pride.

"Who'd you kill, sheriff?" Alice Crapper calls out.

"Lilly Gee."

Gasps of shock and horror fly from every saloon guest, which includes virtually every adult in Dodge City.

I usually wait for murmurs to die down in these sorts of town meetin's, but this time the murmurin' don't die. Finally Laurie Potts yells, "Why'd you kill her?"

While the folks enjoy their murmurin', they'd rather hear the answer to Laurie's question, so they're forced to quiet down.

"She tried to shoot me, and I killed her in self-defense."

The women start yellin' words of outrage to the point if they were armed, I'd be concerned. I wave my hands in the air to try to restore order, while continuin' to speak.

"You knew Lilly Gee as the former Lilly Parker," I shout.

They look around at each other and nod their heads. Yeah, they all knew she was a Parker, from east Texas.

I hold her Bible above my head and say, "This is Lilly's Bible, writ in her own hand, where she admits her actual maiden name was Hartman."

Clair Murphy hollers out, "If her maiden name got her killed, Alice Crapper better head for the hills!"

Everyone laughs or chuckles, 'cept for Alice, and I feel we've passed the worst part.

I know these town folk ain't really makin' sport of one of their friends bein' killed. It's the kind of jokin' you do when you're nervous or in shock. There's also the fact they know my reputation. They were happy when I was sheriff, and I s'pect they're happy to hear I'm back on the job. Or *will* be, after I find Gentry and fetch her home.

I continue my speech: "Lilly was Sam Hartman's sister. Today she asked me to protect her. I told her she could stay here and I'd make sure she was safe. Margaret agreed to bunk with her to keep things proper. Lilly said she'd be here at six, but didn't show, so I went to her place to check on her. When I got there, she tried to shoot me with her rifle, on account of me killin' her brother. I know this is a shock to you, as it was to me, but them are the facts. If anyone wants to dispute my word, speak up now, and we'll discuss it."

"I'd like to see the Bible for myself," Jane Plenty says.

I hand it to her, and Gerta and Louise crowd around her to get a peek. Then I say, "I'd like to conclude this issue, if everyone's satisfied about the way the killin' took place."

"Why are you in such a rush to conclude the issue?" Claire says.

"I need help buryin' her. After that, I aim to go find Gentry."

The people talk among themselves.

Jim Bigsby speaks up. "Emmett...I mean, sheriff?"

"Yes, Jim."

"We ain't got a workin' shovel between us."

"Then I'll need help bringin' her to town. Anyone got a wagon?"

I look around.

"Anyone?"

No one claims ownership of a wagon.

"Jim, with your help I can make a lean-to from the wood we stacked on the floor. We can attach it to one a' these horses, put Lilly's body on it, bring her home, and bury her locally."

"I'm glad to help you, sheriff," Jim says, "but we still don't have a proper shovel."

"We can bury her in my jail hole," I say.

"That's *disgusting!*" May Gray says.

"Well, we could plant her in your garden, if you prefer."

May spins on her heels and stomps out the door, leavin' me to wonder if she ain't as keen on me tonight as she was yesterday.

Everyone starts makin' for the door.

"I have one last piece of business," I say.

They all turn around to hear it. Even May gets word and comes back inside.

"As your duly-sworn sheriff, I hereby appoint Margaret Stallings to be mayor of Dodge City."

The gaspin' about Margaret is nearly as loud as it was for Lilly.

"Why, she's a dang *woman!*" Art Carbunkle shouts.

"She'll end *whorin'*!" George Reed yells.

Everyone looks at George, but only Claire Murphy is rude enough to say, "George, what do you care? You ain't got a poke left in you."

I hold up my hand for quiet, and say, "Margaret has agreed to allow whorin', cussin', gamblin', fightin' and drinkin', 'cause otherwise, how would we build a decent town?"

I see a look on Margaret's face that tells me I worded somethin' wrong, but since no one's throwin' a fit over it, I keep talkin'.

"Margaret has some fine ideas for buildin' a school, a park, a town hall, and other such things."

Except for Claire, the women like the sound of them things, and exchange nods of approval. To them, Margaret represents a step up from our last mayor and town council members, who turned out to be circus performers that snuck into town one night when a nearby circus went bust. But Claire has always been one to stir the pot, and tonight is no exception.

She calls out, "Is this a real job, or is it what you offered Margaret after sharing her bed and jilting her?"

All eyes in the room turn my way.

I say, "Margaret never proposed to me, and I never shared her bed, nor jilted her in any way."

They look at Margaret, who says, "Of all the ridiculous rumors I've heard, this one takes the cake."

"You were seen on one knee in the street proposing to him," Louise says. "Then you jumped up and kissed him flush on the mouth."

Margaret sighs. "I was on one knee to check the locks on Emmett's leg irons. When I realized we had a key to fit the locks, I was so happy for him, yes, I kissed him. If that kiss of happiness for a friend has offended any of you, I humbly apologize."

"You kissed him flush on the *mouth*?" Claire Murphy says.

This is the kind of town Dodge City is. A young, beautiful woman everyone knew has been shot and killed, but an innocent kiss on the mouth is what gets all the attention.

Margaret shakes her head in disgust, and they all look back at me.

"It were a mouth kiss," I concede.

"And there was a second kiss, yes?" May Gray pipes up, causin' me to wish she'd gone home a few minutes earlier.

I give her a frown in response.

"*Was* there a second kiss?" Art says. "We got a right to know what kind a' shenanigans are takin' place behind the walls of justice."

"There was a second kiss," I say. "But it were part of the same happiness expressed at gettin' my leg irons off."

"Just to be clear," Claire says, "Two kisses flush on the mouth, one for each leg cuff?"

"I suppose you could put it that way," I say.

Claire says, "To what shall we attribute the fornicating that took place afterward?"

"Excuse me?"

"It would appear you'd used up all your leg iron joy with the kisses."

"Well, we *did*," I say, tryin' to figure out why it's so much easier to kill women than reason with 'em.

"There was *no fornication!*" Margaret says, raisin' her voice. Then says, "and I resent your insulting accusation. I invited Mr. Love into my home so I could soap the locks. End of story."

"I think there's more story to be had," Claire says.

Margaret sighs. "What else can you *possibly* find to worry about regarding this incident?"

"Did Emmett agree to make you mayor *before*...or *after* the two of you went inside your house?"

"After."

"So you kissed him on the mouth twice, went into the house, removed his leg irons, and his first thought upon being set free was to make you *mayor?*"

The small crowd in the saloon are harrumphin' and callin' out things like "what about that?" and "You expect us to believe that?"

I speak up to defend Margaret's honor, but no one listens till I grab my rifle and rack a bullet into the chamber.

Claire yells, "Run, Alice!"

Alice Crapper yells back, "That weren't funny the first time, Claire."

I fire a warnin' shot into the ceilin'. Then say, "Nothin' happened between Margaret and me. While she was workin' on my leg irons we spoke of what's happened to Dodge.

Margaret expressed ideas of what would help us turn this town into somethin' special. I thought her ideas were good. Since I'm all that's left of the town council, I decided to appoint her mayor. If we can move past this silly conversation, I'd like to give Lilly a proper burial."

"What'll become of her property?" Art says.

"The Hartmans have relatives all over Kansas," I say. "I expect the farm will go to someone whose name is in Lilly's Bible."

"What if they want to claim her body?"

"I'll be glad to let 'em dig it up and get it out of my kitchen."

"While you're off gallivantin' around the country, lookin' for Gentry, how's Margaret gonna enforce the rules?" Tom says.

"She's the mayor. She speaks for the town. If people refuse to abide by reasonable rules, she'll tell me about it when I get back."

"Then what'll happen?"

"It'll be the same as always. If someone breaks the law I take 'em into custody. If they resist, I kill 'em."

The room goes sober, thinkin' about Margaret's power. I soften things by sayin', "Listen, people. There won't be any new rules while I'm gone 'cause there ain't enough town for rules to matter. You should all relax about Margaret bein' mayor. It's not gonna change anythin' around here except for the better."

"A woman mayor?" Tom says. "We'll be a laughin' stock. And mark my words, Emmett. You give a woman an

inch, she'll take a mile. You make this one mayor, and before you know it, the others'll demand the right to vote."

CHAPTER 30

IT TAKES ME and Jim all night to bury Lilly in the jail hole in my kitchen. First we dismantle the lean-to, and throw the wood into the hole over her body. Then we fetch bucket after bucket of dirt from behind the saloon and dump it over her and the wood. In all, we put about four feet of dirt over her. That, plus the wood, should keep the varmints from diggin' her out while I'm gone.

As we finish tampin' down the dirt, I say, "I'm goin' to Springfield."

Jim says, "If Gentry ran off with David Wilkins, they'd go west, not east."

"True, but it's possible my rock-throwin' friend might've helped her and the baby sneak out of town. If he did, they'd a' gone to Springfield, where my friend Rose lives."

"And if they didn't?"

"Rose might have new information to share about Gentry that'll keep me from wastin' my time searchin' the whole damn west with no more to go on than what I have."

"You're not takin' the horses, are you?"

"I aim to."

"But you said the mare won't ride you easterly."

"She won't."

"And the stallion?"

"I hope he will, but who knows?"

"You think the mare will follow you the whole way to Springfield?"

"Margaret? No, I reckon she'll stay here in town."

"Not the mayor, Emmett. The mare."

"Huh?"

"The horse!"

"Oh. Well, I s'pect that mare would follow me to the bowels of hell."

"Why would you make that poor horse walk 400 miles in the heat? I could take good care of her right here."

"Scarlett's a fine mare. I'll offer her to my friend, Rose, in return for two horses and a wagon, so I can fetch Gentry and Scarlett Rose back."

"You think Gentry named your baby after your friend, Rose?"

"I do. She's the only Rose we know. She's got a ranch full of horses in Springfield."

"Maybe she'd sell me a few on credit to help me get back on my feet."

"You been a good friend. I'll bring it up."

"I sure hope you're right about Gentry bein' there."

"That's where she and Scarlett Rose are, I s'pect."

"Is Rose a horse thief?"

"No, of course not!"

"Then why would she accept a stolen horse?"

"I'm not sayin' she will. But she'll be able to tell if the horse's owner is dead."

"How the hell would she know that?"

"I can't say. But I s'pect she'll know, all the same. And if the owner's dead, Rose'll know what to do about it."

"What about the stallion?" Jim says.

"I'll try to ride him to Springfield. If he throws me, I'll walk."

Jim studies my face a minute. Then says, "What if Gentry ain't there, Emmett?"

"Rose'll tell me where to find her."

"And if Rose ain't there to say them words?"

"Her ranch hand, Roberto, will be there, and give me a horse that'll travel in all directions."

"What if the yanks or rebs have burned Rose's house and barn and stolen all her horses?"

I give Jim a stern look. "You paint a bleak picture."

He shrugs.

"It's my way," he says.

"Well, I hope that ain't what I'll find. But if it is, I'll still have Scarlett and possibly the stallion."

"You think she'll ride you back to Dodge?"

"No, but I think she'll bring me six miles north a' Dodge. Then I'll climb off and walk the rest of the way."

"And she'll follow you back to town?"

"That's my guess."

"Why would she do that?"

"It's her way."

CHAPTER 31

OVER THE NEXT four hours I rest as best I can, then sip another cup of birch bark tea, pump enough water to fill the four canteens, saddle both horses, and climb on the stallion. He snorts, and waits for me to dig my heels in his flank. When I do, he starts walkin'. I turn to see what the mare's doin', and find she's standin' by the rail. I wonder if she knows I've untied her. No matter, it's her choice to stay or go, and I won't influence her either way. I face forward and let the stallion have his way, to see what he'll do. My ribs are much improved, but I don't want to chance takin' a spill. He walks to the main trail and turns north.

I cuss and shake my head and brace myself in case he bucks. Then I try to turn him gently eastward. He stops in his tracks and refuses to move. I dig in my heels, but he stands still as a statue. For a long period of time I call him

names I ain't proud to know, then climb off his back, remove the rifle from the scabbard, and start walkin' to
Springfield.

I get a half mile southeast of Dodge before hearin' a
shufflin' sound behind me. I turn to see Scarlett the mare,
followed by Rudy the bear, followed by the stallion. We're
all walkin' in single file, separated by no more than twenty
feet, combined.

The further I walk, the madder I get. I've got two perfectly good horses that refuse to let me ride 'em in the same
direction they're willin' to walk! More than once I stop and
cuss the horses, and even their parents. I ain't one to punish
a horse, but I'll admit to throwin' my hat on the ground and
kickin' hell out of it at least once every mile. And every few
miles I try gettin' on one of the horses. Each time I do, they
turn the opposite way and won't allow me to turn 'em toward Springfield. Of course, that makes me madder than a
hornet, and I start into cussin' some more.

Rudy ain't makin' it any easier. Every time I holler at
the horses he laughs his silly head off. The horses ain't
laughin', but if I didn't know better, I'd swear they're smilin'.

CHAPTER 32

WE'RE WALKIN' THE old Indian trail that leads direct to Springfield, so we're not encounterin' many people. We do see a few, but when they spy Rudy they give us a wide berth. As we pass 'em by they point and stare, and I wonder if these settlers are half as confused as I am angry.

As the day wears on, my pants get baggier and baggier, and I have to keep re-tyin' my rope belt. Salty sweat's runnin' down my crotch and legs and though we're walkin' through grass that's tamped down, it's still thick enough to carry ticks and spiders and chiggers. I don't feel these little beasties till they get to my hands and neck or my privates. Then I shake and hop around and slap 'em off me as best I can, while hollerin' at the horses.

I'm an even-tempered man as long as others have nothin' bad to say about Gentry, but I believe I'm angrier now than at any time in my entire life. Angrier now than when I'd been shot, captured, and forced to work on the Union railroad.

It just don't make sense about these dang horses!

So I keep walkin'.

That night we camp by a stand of trees, where Rudy finds enough tubers to fill his belly.

Last time I traveled this trail, Kansas was goin' through the worst drought in memory, and we nearly thirsted to death. This time there's signs of water to be had when needed, so I know the rivers and ponds'll have enough water to keep Rudy, me, and the horses goin'. As I remove the saddles and saddlebags, I feel bad for cussin' the horses all day. At least they've kept me company. If Shrug and Jim had been walkin' with me all this way I'd a' been grateful for their presence. I wouldn't cuss 'em for not lettin' me ride on their backs.

So I apologize to 'em before fallin' asleep.

Nevertheless, the next mornin' the four of us fall into the same pattern of walkin' to Springfield, and me tryin' to ride the horses there, and them not lettin' me, and me cussin' and throwin' my hat on the ground and kickin' it, and Rudy laughin', and me feelin' bad about it each night and apologizin', and so it goes, day after day. And the thing that makes me cuss the horses each day is the same thing that makes me apologize to 'em each night.

Gentry.

For it's thoughts of seein' her that make me so impatient each mornin', and thoughts of bein' with her that make me so forgivin' each night.

On the ninth night, I can barely contain my enthusiasm. I've thought minute by minute, hour by hour, day by day about the look on Gentry's face when she sees me after all this time. I think about what she'll say, and what it'll feel like to hold her in my arms again. I do realize there's a strong possibility she ain't in Springfield, but I don't dwell on it, 'cause at the worst, I'll see Rose, and she'll have some smart advice to give me about findin' Gentry, and I'll spend a day or so with her, and then head out to find my woman.

And if it turns out she's with another man and they're happy and she don't want to be with me?

That's a thought I don't want to think. And won't, till I'm forced.

In the early mornin' dawn of the tenth day, me, Scarlett, Rudy, and the stallion finally start climbin' the ridge that overlooks Rose's ranch. My heart's poundin' in my chest. I feel the strength of ten men coursin' through my body. It's all I can do not to run up the hill and down the other side, screamin' like a mad man. But that might get me shot by the very woman I love, before I'm close enough for her to recognize me. I realize Gentry ain't seen Rudy in six months, and might appear happier to see him than me. If that's the case, I'll be happy enough, just for havin' made her happy.

Somethin' else I've thought about every day is buildin' up inside me: Not only am I moments away from seein' Gentry, I'm about to meet my daughter!

Me, Scarlett, Rudy, and the stallion climb the last fifty yards to the top of the ridge. Then we stop to look, and I can't believe what I see.

CHAPTER 33

JIM'S WORST THOUGHT is confirmed: Rose's ranch has been burned to the ground. And there ain't a man, woman, child, or horse on the property.

I close my eyes, and fall to my knees. At first, there's nothin' to think. I loved this ranch, and of course it was Rose's dream place. I notice I've been rubbin' my right arm without realizin' it, and silently thank Rose for savin' it at this very ranch a few years back. I came here for a drink of whiskey after a local sawbones, Doc Inman, wanted to cut off my infected arm. Rose didn't give me the whiskey, though she was known for her generosity. Instead, she gave me birch bark tea, and two days later, I paid the doc a visit and thrashed him with the arm he wanted to cut off.

I'm heartbroken at the devastation I see at the bottom of the hill. If this war has got to Rose, the most powerful person I know, then the sufferin' has no limits.

I fall on my back with my eyes still closed, and think about the breakfasts and suppers I've enjoyed at Rose's ranch over the years. I brought all the whores and mail order brides here from Rolla, and Rose always welcomed 'em with food and clothes and kindness. It was here Rose created the poultice that changed Gentry's face from pimply to perfect, and here, where her ranch hand, Roberto, faithfully worked for many years. This is also the one place my friend Shrug could always come and feel safe. He and Rose have an understandin' about things others don't appear to know. Rose calls 'em kindred spirits, though talk of any form of spirits besides whiskey makes me uneasy.

I take a deep breath, and let it out slowly. Then do it again.

I need to re-think my plan.

I knew there was a fair chance Gentry was somewhere else with our baby. But the idea of Rose bein' gone, and her ranch burnt to the ground—never crossed my mind, despite what Jim Bigsby said about it bein' a possibility.

Another deep breath.

Okay.

I think a minute. Rose's ranch is a couple miles west of Springfield. Should I walk there and see if anyone has some useful information? Rose would never live in the town proper, so she ain't likely to be there. Rose ain't the kind to run, or abandon her property without a fight, but the devastation

tation to her ranch is so complete, my guess is, she and Roberto weren't even here when the troops came through.

Rose knows things before they happen.

She probably saw in her brain this was gonna happen, just like she saw the massacre at Lawrence in her mind. I don't know if that ever came to be, but I've never known Rose to be wrong about an event takin' place. So she probably had time to pack up all her household possessions and livestock, and she and Hannah, and Roberto and his wife, and maybe Gentry and Scarlett Rose, and Shrug, all headed somewhere safe from the war, to build a new ranch.

If it happened like that, they won't be in Springfield, nor would they have told anyone of their intentions to pack up and leave, for fear of bein' bushwhacked on their journey.

When I open my eyes, I see both horses on their knees, waitin' for me to climb on whichever back I choose.

I choose Scarlett. When I climb onto the saddle, she stands. She's facin' Springfield, and if that's where she wants to go, I'll be shocked, but I'll let her take me there. I dig in my heels. She spins around and gallops down the hill, headin' in the general direction of Dodge City, with Rudy and the stallion hot on our heels. To anyone who might be watchin', we look like an angry bear is chasin' us across the plains.

After a mile it's clear our pace has created a hardship on Rudy, so I slow down to a walkin' speed where we cover about four miles in each hour. And each hour I swap horses and rest Rudy, so everyone stays fresh.

The first day we do sixteen hours. After that, we travel eighteen hours a day. On the sixth night I'm ridin' the stallion when he starts to angle in a direction that will take us north of Dodge. I try to rein him due west, but he's havin' none of it. I make him whoa, and thank both horses for the ride.

Then I start walkin' the last six miles to Dodge, tryin' to figure how in hell I'm supposed to find an English cattleman, knowin' no more than his name and the fact he lives somewhere north, west, or south of Dodge City, Kansas.

CHAPTER 34

AS USUAL, IT'S me, Scarlett, Rudy, and the stallion walkin' single file to a place the horses won't ride me. I ain't got the strength nor the will to cuss 'em. I've come to the conclusion their behavior is just how it is. It's dark out now, but I keep walkin' anyway. After an hour Rudy comes up behind me and swats me to the ground. He ain't playin' tag this time, he's expressin' his hunger. He's traveled with me enough to know we're supposed to stop at dusk and dig for tubers.

"I'm hungry too," I say out loud. "But I aim to sleep in my bed tonight."

A few minutes later he swats me again, so I open the saddlebags and give him the last of the tubers he'd dug the first night, more'n two weeks ago.

The horses have been chewin' grass along the trail since the moment I climbed off the stallion's back. I can't actually see Rudy anymore, but I know where he's lyin' and what he's poutin' about.

"I miss her too."

He lets out a mournful cry, and I say, "We'll find her, I promise." I take three steps in his direction, aimin' to give him a reassurin' hug, but trip over somethin' and barely keep my balance. I let out a small curse and reach back behind me to see what nearly did me in.

A large rock.

And that puts a thought in my head.

An hour later the four of us enter the *Spur*. I unsaddle the horses, draw some well water into a bucket, and leave the bucket on the floor for them to drink. Then I head wearily upstairs, climb in my bed, and sleep until I hear Gentry's voice askin', "Please Emmett, just a few more minutes?"

I bolt up in bed and realize I'd been dreamin' of a time, long ago, when Gentry and me were layin' on a hilltop, side by side, and I wanted to get up and eat breakfast. She wanted some extra time with me, and I kept tryin' to rush her along. That same mornin' her friend Scarlett was gored by a mad bull.

Thinkin' back on it now, I can't believe there was ever a time I had Gentry layin' beside me, beggin' me to stay with her just a few more minutes, and didn't properly appreciate the wonderfulness of that opportunity. God knows if I could do it again, I wouldn't leave her side for breakfast, or even supper.

But that's the sadness of life. You never truly appreciate what you've got till you lose it. Other things seem more important at the time.

But they ain't.

I sigh, then climb out of bed, put on my clothes, walk down the stairs, and out the front door. Last night I tripped over a rock and realized my best friend and former scout, Shrug, would never have left town without givin' me a sign about how to find him. All those months we worked together, Shrug scouted the area miles in front of me, and left direction stones for me to follow. He always used five stones. He'd place four stones to show north, south, east and west, with the fifth stone pointin' the direction I was supposed to go. I never got in trouble when I followed the stones.

I spend the entire day walkin' up and down each trail that leads out of Dodge, lookin' for the stones Shrug might've left for me. Around four in the afternoon, I find 'em.

Problem is they've been scattered, and I can't tell which direction I was supposed to go.

I'm flustered, but not about to give up. Because if Shrug left these stones, there'll be another set a few miles away So all I have to do is travel up to five miles from this spot on every trail till I find another pile of stones. Even if that pile is scattered, I'll know I'm headin' in the right direction.

This ain't an easy way to follow a person, and it takes me three full days to exhaust all the possibilities. But I finally do, and eventually have to face the fact I've misread his sign.

Or maybe them five stones was a coincidence, and the ones Shrug set out for me are closer to town.

I go back to Dodge and look everywhere for stones Shrug might've left for me to follow. Hit every street, every path. But if he laid stones for me, they're long gone. Some kid picked 'em up for his slingshot, or they got kicked out of place, or crushed by horses or oxen. Here and there I run into some of the Dodge widows, who offer me coffee or lemonade. When I decline they give me a look of sympathy. Some shake their heads and tell me they hope I'll find Gentry. Others just shake their heads. I know they think I'm pitiful, but true love will do this to folks.

The hardest part of this search is knowin' ahead of time Gentry left with either Wilkins or Shrug. If she left with Wilkins, there'd be no stones. If Shrug, they'd have traveled away from the main trails, which means the stones would be covered by six months of grass and weather.

In other words, I'm wastin' my time.

But since I got no better ideas, I keep walkin' circles around Dodge, tryin' to search out any type of clue that could help me. But clues, like direction stones, are nowhere to be found. While searchin', I think thoughts about Wilkins, Gentry, and Shrug.

And none of the thoughts are good.

It's hot today, and I'm in a foul mood. I need to go someplace peaceful, to sort out my thoughts. I notice Jim Bigsby's livery and barn nearby, and head there. The livery's quiet and shady, but it ain't a place for reflectin' on things. I cross the road to Jim's barn, push open the front door, and see a truly beautiful view on the far end, where Jim's left the tall door open. I spot a length of rope looped around a post hook that brings back a memory of a time when I was a boy, and my only possessions beyond my clothes were a slingshot and a well-formed cowboy rope like this one. I remove it from the hook and dust it off and work it in my hands to help me think.

It's a cowboy thing.

You wouldn't understand.

I hold onto one end and toss the rest on the floor, and make it dance in circles by spinnin' my wrist. I make it look like three large spinnin' wheels. Then I work it side to side, till it slides across the floor like a thirty-foot snake. Eventually, I coil it and hold it in my right hand and walk to the end of the barn that has the nice view, and lean against the left side of the doorway. I look out onto the giant field below me, that's part green, part yellow, a sign of a generally mild summer in Dodge.

But what's really special is the sky.

Vast and deep blue it is, with nary a cloud. As I stand in the doorway, a slight breeze cools my face, and I begin reflectin' on the thoughts I had, that Gentry is almost certainly with the English cattleman, David Wilkins, and if she is, I hope and pray she's with him by choice.

Because if she's not, my best friend Shrug is dead.

CHAPTER 35

I BELIEVE THE story about Wilkins fallin' in love with Gentry. And I s'pect she liked him, too, as a friend, since she went straight out the next day and cut a Christmas tree and decorated it. I s'pect she showed him her tree, and maybe he even helped her decorate it, which galls me, thinkin' how he might've put his hands on the strips of fabric that used to be part of her fine dress. I also believe he snuck back into town to try talkin' her into marryin' him and livin' on his ranch. Bein' fearful, lonely, and havin' uncertain finances, she'd have listened to him. All the town women were losin' husbands and sons to the war, and Gentry would've seen their deep sadness. Then the bank got robbed, almost certainly by Wilkins and his men, and she likely lost what savin's she might've had. While all this was happenin', Scarlett Rose was brand new in the world, and Gentry must've

Gentry must've been terrified wonderin' how to provide for her on her own, what with the saloon goin' broke.

Over the months he probably kept comin' back, puttin' more and more pressure on her, after she closed the saloon and let the whores go. A rich cattleman like David Wilkins is probably used to gettin' his way and ain't likely to give up easily. He'd want the sort of woman who'd appear impossible to get. But I s'pect Gentry held firm, and at some point Wilkins threatened her.

And that's when she would've snuck out of town with Shrug, or finally given in to David Wilkins's proposal of marriage.

But if Gentry had snuck out with Shrug, he would've put Rudy in the woods and then taken Gentry and the baby someplace safe, like wherever Rose is livin' with her adopted daughter, Hannah. But if Shrug had done that, he would've come back to look for me, and leave fresh stones for me to follow.

But there ain't no fresh stones, which means Gentry went with Wilkins peacefully. Because there's no way in hell Shrug would have allowed Wilkins to steal Gentry. He'd a' left stones for me to follow, and would a' died tryin' to protect Gentry.

And maybe that's what happened.

Or maybe Gentry and the baby and Shrug snuck out of town and he took them to wherever Rose is, and when he came back to find me, he got killed, or captured like I did. Maybe he's bein' forced to build a railroad somewhere.

That's possible, but it ain't what I feel in my heart.

I feel like I'm missin' somethin'.

I work the rope around in my hand some more, enjoyin' the feel of it. It's an old rope, but still lively, thanks to the fact it's been kept indoors. Had it been outdoors even a few months, it'd be a worthless lump.

At that moment, standin' at the far end of the barn lookin' out over that beautiful field and gorgeous sky, I suddenly realize what I'd been missin' about Shrug and the stones.

CHAPTER 36

SHRUG WOULD A' known his stones couldn't stay in place on a trail over time. Hundreds of travelers and livestock would have traveled these trails and grass patches over the past six months. Not to mention Dodge is the windiest city I ever seen. If people and animals didn't destroy the rocks, windstorms, hail storms, and twisters would've scattered 'em.

Shrug would've known stones wouldn't work.

But big, heavy boulders would.

I wonder if maybe Shrug rolled some boulders or heavy rocks somewhere near the edge of town that were so big they couldn't be affected by people or nature. Could I have walked right past a cluster of boulders without even noticin'?

Of course I could! When a man's pannin' for gold dust, he don't see the sand in the pan. I bet there's a cluster of five giant rocks somewhere that are too big to trip over. And I probably passed them several times while lookin' for somethin' smaller.

Since I'm lookin' for giant rocks 'stead of small stones, it'd make sense to start my search by climbin' onto the roof of the tallest buildin' in town, which happens to be the *Spur*. I put Jim's rope back on the hook and move quickly to my old saloon. Once there, I climb the back stairs to the landin', stand on the rail, and pull myself up onto the roof. My plan is to stand and scan the horizon for giant rocks, but I don't get around to doin' that, because there are stones on my roof.

They're scattered, but it's clear there ain't four stones, and there ain't six.

There's five.

I stand to my full height and can see several rooftops from here, all of which have stones on 'em!

I remember Jim tellin' me Shrug used to hide on these roofs and chunk rocks at people who were tryin' to hurt Rudy. But the roofs I can see from this position all have exactly five stones on 'em. I'm feelin' no small excitement as I run and jump from roof to roof and discover Shrug has left five stones on every rooftop in town, hopin' at least one pile would survive in place.

But none did.

I'm on the last roof of the last buildin' in town. In frustration, I kick a rotten roof board loose, and almost fall into the attic space of what used to be Patti's Pie Kitchen. My leg goes through, and I feel a hot burst of steamy air come through and my first thought is *How the hell was Shrug able to survive in our attic?*

Attic?

Then it hit me. Shrug didn't expect them stones to survive the elements. He was tryin' to get me to look in the attics.

I start with the Pie Kitchen attic.

And find five stones. A north, south, east and west stone, with a fifth one pointin' northwest. What's northwest of here?

Colorado Territory.

Why's that significant?

Because Huerfano County starts just beyond the Kansas border. And Huerfano County is often called *Cattle County*, since the biggest ranches in the west are located there!

My heart soars like it has wings. I go next door, kick my way into the attic of the abandoned dry goods store and find five stones with the fifth stone pointin' north-west.

I go back to *The Lucky Spur*, and enter the attic. And see five stones with the fifth one pointin' north-west. And find somethin' else: a small, leather book with writin' in it. It's dark in here, so I bust a board off the roof so I can read the words:

Emmett, first thing is yore a fother! Our baby girl is Scarlett Rose. I love you with all my hart. If you find this you will no times have become desprit for us. Shrug saved me over and over and was going to take us to a safe playse but took Rudy to the woods first and never came back. I feer he is killed. Emmett I am a city girl. I cant raze our baby in the woods by myself. Ten cowboys cood find me inside a day. Times are hard and my milk dryed up. I did all I cood but must think of Scarlett Rose.

Try not to be mad at this next part. Try hard.

Soon I will have to do bad things like I did before. I will do thoze things to keep your child alive and safe. I hope you will forgive me. If you love me you will no I held out till there was no other choyse.

O Emmett where are you? I know you are alive. Before Rose disapeered she sed she will send a horse to bring you to me. I wate every day for you and that dam horse.

Dont you still want me?

If not pleeze tell me to my face so you can hold your sweet child. Pleeze want me in your famly. I did all I cood to be your good girl frend.

Well this is the most words I rote since I terned 12 & got sold to the hore house, so I will end with this. I love you Emmett. Now come find me!

CHAPTER 37

I'M STANDIN' HERE in the attic feelin' like the dumbest man that ever lived. Two weeks ago I'm lyin' in a field, nearly dead from an Indian attack, and a horse shows up out of nowhere. A horse that happens to be carryin' everythin' I need to survive. A horse that would only travel in one direction. But I'm so bull-headed, it don't even cross my mind this horse was sent by Rose to take me straight to Gentry's arms. I shake my head in disgust, thinkin' how I wasted all this time, and worry what terrible things Gentry might've had to do these past two weeks I could've spared her from doin'.

I head straight for Jim Bigsby's house with Scarlett, Rudy, and the stallion followin' close behind. When Jim comes out I give him the stallion, to repay him for his kindness and hard work. I add in the saddle that came with it, and the saddlebags, though I need the canteens for my trip. I ask if he'll keep Rudy in one of his stalls till I get back, since I can't have him followin' me to wherever Gentry might be waitin'. Jim agrees, so we take the stallion and Rudy to the livery and put 'em in stalls. Then I practice shootin' my new rifle, and find it to be the most accurate one I ever used. I re-load it, and put the box of bullets in my pocket, check my canteens, climb on Scarlett's back, and hit the trail.

CHAPTER 38

SCARLETT THE HORSE ain't wastin' time. In fact, she's runnin' so fast I can barely hang on. When she realizes I'm gonna let her go in the direction she pleases, she slows to a reasonable speed. Three hours into the trip, I give her a small tug and she stops so I can climb off. We're twenty miles northwest of Dodge, and this appears to be a good place to make camp.

But I ain't makin' camp.

Though I don't know the area well, I've got a horse that does, and I aim to let her ride me all through the night, if that's her choice.

After stretchin' my legs a minute, and gettin' out-pissed by Scarlett, I climb back on, and she takes me across the moonlit plains.

We stop for breakfast, and I try to cipher how far we've come. My best guess is sixty miles, which puts us half-way to Colorado, or there-abouts. After a brief stretch, we continue due west. Around noon I whoa my horse long enough to shoot a jackrabbit. My plan is to eat it for dinner, but my appetite gets the better of me, and I fry him up around three in the afternoon. I figure it don't matter much, since I'll probably be ridin' all night anyway.

I do ride all through the night again, and as usual, my thoughts turn to Gentry. I wonder things like what she's doin', and if she's bein' mistreated by Wilkins. Her letter said *try not to be mad*. Well, of course I ain't mad! Gentry's doin' what she has to do to stay alive and keep our baby safe. I'm touched it were such a hard decision for her to make. Here's a woman that whored from the age of twelve to seventeen. She could've run off with this wealthy feller way back in December of 1861, but didn't. She waited for me. We weren't even married, and she waited for me. She had my baby, lost her business, and kept waitin' for me. The bank got robbed, she lost her money, and she waited for me. Wilkins came back for her time and again, promisin' God knows what, and still she waited for me. When he threatened her, she made plans to run off with Shrug to a safe place rather than spread her legs for this man who seems willin' to marry her and care for her and the baby. The fact that Gentry tried so hard not to fall back into a life where she gives her pleasures to a man for money shows how much she loves me. And when a woman loves a man like that, nothin' should make me mad or keep us separated.

I don't fault David Wilkins for any part of what he done except the threatenin'. That's the part that don't sit right with me. I can't hardly blame a man for fallin' in love with Gentry, since I done the same thing myself. But a man who'll threaten a woman into givin' up her charms, and won't take no for an answer, well, that's the sort of man who needs his pecker shot off.

When I ain't wonderin' them types of thoughts I wonder other things like is this the same way Gentry traveled six months ago? I doubt it, since we ain't followin' a trail, and she and the baby would've likely been on a buckboard. But I pay close attention to all that's around me, just in case. Because it comforts me thinkin' she might've smelled the same scent of pine in the distance, or traveled over the same dry, cracklin' grass. I look at the moon and wonder if, wherever she is, could she be lookin' at it right now? I have a picture in my mind where she's in Wilkins's huge ranch house, sleepin' upstairs in his bed, when she hears our baby cry in the next room. She slips out without wakin' him up, and holds Scarlett Rose while sittin' on the window box in the upstairs bedroom, starin' out the window, lookin' for a skinny man on a white horse.

The next mornin' I cross a thick, fast-movin' crick and find myself in a beautiful clearin' that's open in the center, with a thick stand of trees and juniper bushes on either side. A thin, purple line of mountains can be seen in the far distance above and below a pale blue sky. As I stand in my stirrups to let the water drain down my pant legs, a shot rings out.

Scarlett the horse staggers and falls to the ground, and breathes her last breath.

CHAPTER 39

BY STAGGERIN', SCARLETT gave me just enough time to react. I push out of my stirrups and fall to the ground behind her. I scramble back toward her quickly and lie beside her, hopin' to make myself a smaller target. Unfortunately, me and Scarlett are lyin' on the riverbank, which makes me a sittin' duck. I look around, but see no smoke to show where the gun was that shot my horse. Nor do I see any cover I can run to without gettin' shot. I reach into the scabbard and pull my rifle free and prepare to shoot.

But nothin' happens.

As seconds turn to minutes, I decide if someone meant to kill me, they could a' done so several times. But just as I'm about to stand, I catch a glimpse of somethin' flashin' in a bush by the trees a hundred yards to my right. It were just an instant flash, then nothin'. But it's enough for me to target, so I set my aim at the top of a four foot bush near the base of a tree and pull the trigger.

Nothin'.

I aim two feet lower and shoot again, and hear someone cry out in pain. I feel a tug in my hat as a bullet catches the tip and passes through, just missin' my skull. That shot came from the opposite side, where the grass is three feet high. There's no wind, so I know the slight movement of the grass was caused by someone lowerin' his rifle. I jump to my feet and put a bullet right where I know he has to be, and he don't scream, but I see a burst of red fan out above the grass.

I'm powerful sad for Scarlett, and the only happy thought is she didn't suffer. My next thought's a selfish one, that I'm goin' to have a devil of a time findin' Gentry now. But at least I know the direction we've been headin'. If I keep walkin', I'll eventually find people, and when I do, I'll ask about David Wilkins. If he's a big-time rancher, he's bound to have land nearby.

I give Scarlett a hug and thank her for all she done for me, and silently apologize for all the times I cussed her last week. Then I busy myself with tryin' to pull the saddlebags out from under her body. It's hard, noisy work, and I don't see the group of cowboys movin' in on me until it's too late.

CHAPTER 40

THERE'S NINE OF 'em, and they've got the drop on me. I look at my rifle propped against Scarlett's body. It's only four feet away, but that's as good as a mile when six pistols and three rifles are pointin' at me.

I say, "You shot my horse."

No one speaks, so I say, "I'm sheriff of Dodge City. If you'll kindly tell me where David Wilkins's ranch is, I won't arrest you this time."

Most of 'em snicker, but the one that's in charge motions me to drop the saddlebags. I do, and they close in on me. Several point their guns at my face, while another ties my hands behind my back. Then they lead me a half mile through some scrub brush till we come to an open area where I see four circus cages in a line. It's clear they were brightly painted at one time, but seem to have taken a beatin' from the elements. It's also clear they once held wild animals.

The cowboys lift me off the ground and push me into the front cage, then hitch a team of oxen to it, and start travelin' in the same direction Scarlett had been takin' me.

As the oxen start movin', the wagon groans and creaks to life. The wheels haven't been oiled for years, it appears, based on the frightful noise they're makin'. While we roll over the hard-packed dirt, I test the bars of the cage, hopin' to find 'em weakened with age. I can't budge 'em, nor can I slide my body between the bars.

I can't see him, but I know there's one cowboy up front, drivin' the wagon, and three others I can see, all on horseback. One is on the right, one on the left, and the third is in the back, followin' at a short distance. I notice another rider movin' on up ahead. He's probably goin' to scout us to wherever we're headin'.

Four cowboys remain at the river bank available to shoot the next horse that comes along.

CHAPTER 41

Bowie County, Texas
Rose & Shrug, Two Weeks Earlier...

ROSE KNEW SHRUG was heading her way. When he crossed Tuck Crick she was on the other side, waiting for him. After a long hug, she gave him a bottle of whiskey and said, "I'll apologize in advance for the language I'm bound to use over the next few minutes."

Shrug smiled and took a pull of his whiskey.

"I'm not one to interfere," she said, "but this bullshit has gone too far!"

Shrug nodded, but Rose couldn't tell if he was agreeing with her or simply showing his approval of the whiskey.

She said, "Emmett was too pig-headed to realize the horse would take him to Gentry, so he lost two full weeks, during which time Gentry decided to stop fornicating with Wilkins."

She waited for Shrug to respond, but instead he took another pull.

Rose said, "They locked you in the animal cage six months ago."

He nodded.

"You could've got out anytime you wanted to, but instead you remained inside the cage so you could be near Gentry."

Shrug shrugged.

"Then you sensed what was about to happen, and came to see if I'd help."

He nodded.

"Like I don't have enough to do here."

Shrug put his hands in front of him like he was rocking a baby.

Rose said, "The baby's fine. Faith named him Jed, after her brother that died as an infant. He's a wild little thing, and it's all I can do to keep him in sight, now that he's got use of his legs."

Shrug made his symbol for a woman.

"Faith is doing well, though she's bored. She went through a bad spell last year when Bose Rennick went back to the house looking for her and killed her parents."

Shrug raised his eyebrows.

"No, I didn't see it coming," Rose said. "I don't see as much of the future as you think I do, but I swear, that Bose Rennick's a hard case. If ever a man needed killing, it's him.

Though it's not my destiny to kill him, I might turn him into a beaver."

Shrug held his nose.

"A skunk?"

Shrug nodded.

"Fine. I'll turn him into a skunk. Or would, if I were a witch."

Shrug cocked his head.

Rose smiled.

"We'll see," she said. "Anyway, I've sown the seeds for romance. Jed and Scarlett Rose will meet in Dodge City in her fourteenth year. They'll fall in love the moment their eyes meet, and I'll deliver their baby the following year. I've erased Faith's memory of having Bose's baby or hearing Emmett's name, so she won't be a deterrent to the romance."

Shrug pretended to pull a gun, his symbol for Emmett. Then he rocked a pretend baby.

Rose shook her head. "No, I'm afraid Emmett won't live to see his grandchild."

Shrug lowered his head, then looked up at her with an angry expression.

Rose said, "Emmett's going to die in two weeks. In a lion cage."

Shrug shook his head side to side.

Rose said, "He and Gentry fulfilled their destiny by having the baby. I love them dearly, and tried to help. I sent horses, food, weapons, and gold. I sent a key to open the locks on his leg irons. I did my best."

Shrug shook his head again, more forcefully.

"Out of the question," she snapped. "It's destiny."

He put the cork back in his bottle and threw it on the ground. Then turned his back to her.

Rose frowned as she watched him head back to the crick. "Look, I know he's your best friend. I like him, too. But I can't just go around keeping people alive just because we *like* them."

He stopped, turned, and gave her a stern look.

She sighed.

CHAPTER 42

Huerfano County, Colorado
Gentry & David, Present Day...

"COME, DARLING," DAVID Wilkins said. "I've something to show you in the barn."

Gentry set her jaw, but said nothing.

"You won't want to miss this," he said.

"I'm not interested," Gentry said. "It's time to feed Scarlett."

"She'll be fine."

Gentry frowned, but reminded herself not to be too strident. Though she loathed the man, Wilkins was generally peaceful, as long as she kept him serviced. But three weeks ago she made the mistake of talking back to him. He struck her, blacking her eye, and she'd withheld her charms ever since. He'd felt bad for striking her, and had given her this time to cool off, but his mood had grown steadily sour as a result, and Gentry knew the next beating was right around the corner.

With this in mind, she kept the anger out of her voice, while keeping it steady, and firm. "I'm afraid I have to insist on feeding Scarlett Rose."

She expected his eyes to narrow into slits of fury, but instead they twinkled, as if he were delighted about something. This was a new emotion, and it gave her pause.

He said, "Come to the barn."

"I think not," she said.

He lashed out and cuffed the side of her head, knocking her onto the bed. Then he jumped on the bed next to her, spun her around, and pushed her face into the mattress. He put his knee against her back and dug it into her spine.

Gentry yelped in pain and tried to shake him off. He removed his knee, but held her down with his left hand while pulling her dress up with his right. Then he spanked her bottom as if punishing a wayward child. Suddenly, he stopped. Gentry could tell he was staring at her, and she knew what that meant.

"You can come with me to the barn, or I can pull your knickers down and give it to you in the arse," he said. "Your choice."

"The barn," Gentry said. "But allow me to relieve myself first. Please."

Wilkins gave her knickers a long look before saying, "Very well, then."

CHAPTER 43

Barn, Wilkins Ranch
Emmett Love, Present Day...

I'VE BEEN IN the cage since yesterday mornin'. Ain't sure where I am, 'cause after knockin' me cold with a gun butt, someone covered the top and sides of the cage with canvass. I'm pretty sure I'm under a roof, though, and if I were guessin', I'd say I'm in a large barn. I smell hay and hear birds flyin' back and forth overhead, as if they're trapped, lookin' for a way to escape. Me and the birds have that much in common.

I'm thinkin' slowly, like I'm in a fog. Improvin' steadily, but my brain ain't quite a hundred percent yet. 'Course, my head's on fire from the blow I took. I reach up and feel the knot with my fingertips, touchin' the dried blood to get an idea how badly I'm hurt.

Other than a severe headache and brain fog, I seem to be okay.

I get to my feet and reach between the bars and grab some of the canvass fabric and try to pull it down so I can see what I'm up against.

But the canvass don't move.

I'm about to call out when I hear a heavy door slide open. Then I hear a man's voice speakin' with a funny accent. I've heard that type of accent before. It's the kind English people have.

He says, "Darling, we're going to play a little game."

I move closer to that side of the cage so I can hear him better. At first I wait to see if the person called darlin' was gonna speak, but no one does, so he says, "There are two cages in front of you. Hank?"

"Sir?" a man says.

"Would you be so kind as to remove the canvasses?"

"Yes, sir."

The canvasses are removed and I see a man who I take to be David Wilkins, standing beside a beautiful woman who's wearin' a gorgeous sorrel-colored dress that runs from the middle of her neck to the toes of her black boots.

It's Gentry.

She's rubbin' the side of her head, as if it's hurtin' her. I'm so stunned, I can't speak. She hasn't noticed me yet, she's too busy starin' at the other cage, screamin', "Take her out of that cage this *instant!*"

I follow her gaze to the other cage and see a baby girl sittin' in the middle of it, surrounded by bars. The baby looks at Gentry and starts clappin' her hands.

"You haven't seen the other cage yet, my love," Wilkins says, calmly.

He points at me. Gentry follows his gesture, sees me, and faints dead away.

"You *bastard!*" I yell.

"I'll ignore that for the moment," Wilkins says, producin' something from his pocket he puts under Gentry's nose. Two seconds later, she comes to with a start.

"*Emmett!*" she yells. She scrambles to her feet and tries to run to my cage, but the man I take to be Hank aims his rifle at me and fires a shot that knocks the hat off my head. It's a helluva shot, the way it hit my hat while missin' my head by a fraction of an inch, and missed the cage bars, as well. I could duplicate that shot, but there ain't many of us that could. On the other hand, that's the second hole shot into my hat in two days, and I prefer a hat with no holes.

Gentry stops in her tracks and screams, thinkin' I've been shot.

"I'm okay!" I yell.

"That was a warning shot," Hank says to Gentry. "Back on up now, Miss, or pick flowers for his funeral."

She searches my eyes, making sure I'm truly okay. When she sees I am, she backs up without taking her eyes off me. "I'm so, so sorry, Emmett," she says, cryin'.

It hurts my heart to hear the pain in her voice.

In a mockin' tone, Wilkins says to Gentry, "So this is the great sheriff of Dodge City I've heard so much about. The great Emmett Love, father of your bastard child, love of your life. Would you like me to release him?"

"Yes!" Gentry says. She turns to face Wilkins and adds, meekly, "Would you? Please, David."

"Did you hear that, Hank? She said please!"

Wilkins turns back to Gentry and says, "If I let Emmett go, would that finally make you happy?"

"Yes."

He nods, as if thinkin' about it. Then says, "What's it worth to you?"

She looks him in the eye. "If you set him free, I'll do anything you say."

"Anything?"

"Yes."

"Would you agree to never see him again, as long as you live?"

"Yes."

"I don't believe you."

"*Please!*" She looks at me.

"I'm okay," I say, unable to take my eyes off her.

To my amazement, Gentry looks more beautiful than ever. Last time I saw her she was seventeen. Now she's twenty, and blossomed into womanhood, and motherhood, and it suits her. I notice tears streamin' down her cheeks. Every time Wilkins looks away she mouths the words, "I love you! I love you so much!" and also, "I'm so sorry!"

Wilkins says, "I hate to interrupt this heartfelt reunion, but all games come with a set of rules, and this one is no exception. Mr. Love, the rules of courtesy require me to compliment your extraordinary taste in women. Over the past six months I've thoroughly enjoyed tasting every inch of Gentry, including her naughty bits. I've also made fucking the living piss out of her part of my daily ritual."

He studies my face to see how I'll respond.

I've been told my mother used to say if a man can't say somethin' nice, he should say nothin' at all. So I don't.

Then he says, "Of course, I can do anything I want to her, since she's my legal wife."

He sees the stunned expression on my face, and laughs.

"Oh, you didn't *know* that? Well, now you do. It's a fact she can't deny."

He turns his attention to Gentry, who's starin' at the ground in shame and embarrassment. Then he says, "But Gentry's been a bit chilly toward me of late. While I'm fond of her physicality, her insolence is more than I can bear. I'll cut to the chase. I'm willing to return her to you, if such is her wish."

"*Yes!*" Gentry says. "That's my wish."

"Sincerely?"

"Yes. More than anything!"

"Is that all you have to say to me?" he says.

She raises her eyes toward his and says, "Thank you, David. I will always remember you kindly, for doing this."

Wilkins laughs. "Don't thank me quite so quickly, my love. Remember, we're playing a game."

"I-I don't understand," Gentry says.

"The game is simple. There are two cages. Your baby's in one, her father's in the other. You get to choose one of them. The one you choose will live. The one you reject will be tortured and killed while you watch."

CHAPTER 44

"WHAT?" GENTRY SCREAMS. "*Oh my God! You wouldn't!*"

"I would and I will," he says. "Make no mistake."

"I won't choose between them!" she says.

"In that case, I'll kill them both."

"*No!*"

"The clock is ticking, my love. You have my word. I'll spare one of them, and kill the other."

"You don't *understand!*"

"Oh, but I do, beloved."

"If you truly love me, as you say, you'll spare them both."

He gives her a puzzled look. "I will?"

She nods. "It would please me greatly."

He says, "Really! Hmm. Well, in that case I suppose I don't love you as much as I thought, since I absolutely intend to kill one of them in three minutes."

"*Please!*"

"Choose."

"I-I can't. Please don't make me. Please don't."

"I'll kill them both. You *know* I will."

"Gentry!" I holler. "Save Scarlett Rose."

She looks at me. "I can't live without you, Emmett. I just *can't*."

"I've lived a long, happy life, and I got to see you one last time. I can die happy." I point to Scarlett Rose. "That's our *baby*! She's got a right to a long, happy life, too. Please, Gentry, it ain't a hard decision at all."

I look at the guy holdin' a rifle. "Are you Hank?"

He looks at Wilkins. Wilkins looks amused. "Yes, that's Hank. What of it?"

"Hank, if you've got an ounce of decency you'll shoot me right now. Give the order, Wilkins, I'm eager to go."

Hank looks at his boss again.

Wilkins says, "Two minutes." Then adds, "Emmett, if Gentry chooses the baby, Hank will shoot your feet and hands first, then your crotch. Then Gentry, Scarlett, and I will watch you bleed to death."

"*No!*" Gentry says.

Wilkins produces a coin from his pocket.

"Shall I flip a coin, then?"

Gentry falls to her knees, clasps her hands in front of her chest. "Please," she says. "Don't do this, David."

"Tell me I've won," he says.

"You've won."

"Tell me I'm better than him."

She pauses.

"*Say it!*" Wilkins shouts.

"You're better than him," Gentry says. "You're better than all of us. Please, David, show mercy. Let Emmett go."

"Kiss my foot," Wilkins says.

She lays her full body on on the barn floor and kisses his boot.

"Lick it."

She does.

"What will you do if I agree to spare your precious Emmett?"

"Anything."

"You're a lying whore!" he says, spitting the words.

"I'm *not* lying! I'll do anything."

"Will you eat a horse turd?"

"Yes."

He laughs. "Of course you would. And so would I. It'd be an improvement on your cooking."

Despite the terrible situation we're in, I have to agree with Wilkins on that point, havin' tasted Gentry's cookin' in the past. I'd a' thought after all this time she'd have gotten better at it, but I suppose good cookin' ain't a skill that comes natural to all women.

"Time's up," Wilkins says.

"*Please!*" Gentry shrieks.

"Heads, baby lives. Tales, Emmett."

"*No!*"

He flips the coin in the air...

CHAPTER 45

THE COIN GOES up about three feet, spinnin' all the while, then stops in mid air. I mean, it's still spinnin', but it ain't fallin'. It's just suspended in the air, spinnin' around and around.

Everyone's fixated on it, except Gentry, who pulls a derringer from her garter belt and shoots Hank with one barrel, and Wilkins with the other. Both men fall to the floor. Neither is dead, but Wilkins is worse. Hank sees his rifle six feet away, and starts slidin' across the floor, tryin' to retrieve it.

I holler, "Gentry!" and point at Hank.

Gentry removes Wilkins's gun from its holster and casually walks over and puts a bullet into Hank's head. Then she picks up his rifle, brings it to me, and fishes it through the bars of my cage.

I'm tryin' to speak, but Gentry puts a finger over her lips and says, "Be right back."

She walks over to Wilkins, who's writhin' on the hard-packed dirt floor.

"Are you in pain, love?" she says, lookin' at his bloody crotch.

He's gaspin' for air, while moanin' low, like a wounded animal. He nods. Yep, he's in pain.

"Good," Gentry says. Then adds, "We're going to play a little game, love."

The coin is still spinnin' in the air, so I say a silent thank you to Rose. As if respondin', the door of the cage slides open. I jump out and rush past Gentry, to the door, ready to shoot however many cowboys might be headin' our way.

But there ain't none.

I mean, there are more than a dozen cowboys in the yard, racin' toward the barn, it's just that they're frozen like statues. I walk over to Scarlett Rose's cage and tug on the door and it opens easily. I put the rifle down and scoop my baby in my arms and hold her close to my cheek, which makes her cry. Probably my whiskers from not havin' shaved since the night May Gray pulled my pecker. I mean, gave me a shave and haircut.

I lower the baby and cradle her in my arms and rock her while hearin' Gentry say, "Kiss my foot."

I don't want to imply Gentry has a cruel streak, nor will I interrupt her, since she's got six months of abuse to settle with Wilkins. I move past her with the baby, into the open area that surrounds the barn.

"Now lick it," Gentry says to Wilkins, as I carry Scarlett Rose across the yard toward the house, where I expect to find enough money to rebuild the town of Dodge City, Kansas.

With the new mayor's approval, I'd like to relocate the town ten miles north, which would put us a scant two miles from the east-west trail.

A single shot rings out from the direction of the barn.

I can't think of anyone who'd object to movin' their home ten miles north, 'cept possibly May Gray, who loves her house and garden more than any woman I ever met. Of course, when Gentry hears about the kind of shave and haircuts May Gray offers, ten miles is probably a smart distance to keep between 'em.

We're in the upstairs bedroom. I set Scarlett Rose on the floor and find her a toy to play with. What I'm lookin' for is a safe, but what I find is an enormous wooden box built into the wall behind a huge paintin'. I pull the paintin' from the wall and prop it against the night stand. When I open the box, I gasp at the riches that lay within. As I start removin' sacks of gold coins from the box, I look up and see Gentry standin' in the doorway, wearin' a smile as big as Texas.

I smile back.

"You don't have to steal his money," she says, holdin' up her hand.

At first, I don't understand. Then she wiggles her fingers till I see the sparkle comin' off her wedding ring.

"This is all ours now," she says.

I point at the box.

She nods.

I point at the room, and outside the window.

She nods again. "As far as the eye can see, all ours."

She removes the wedding ring and places it in the drawer of a narrow table by the door. Then starts unbuttonin' her dress. "And *this*," she says...

I point to her.

She nods, and darts behind the dressin' curtain.

Within seconds it looks like a cyclone hit a clothin' store as all sorts of duds come flyin' out from behind it, includin' frilly underthin's. Lots and lots of frilly underthin's.

Then a pause, and one final frilly underthin'.

Then her left leg kicks out from behind the dressin' curtain. Then her right hand appears over the top and her finger beckons me to come.

"This is all yours, Emmett!"

Not that I mind bein' wealthy, but I'd give up everythin' that's in the box for what's behind the curtain.

THE END

Special Offer from John Locke!

If you like my books, you'll LOVE my mailing list! By join-
ing, you'll receive discounts of up to 67% on future eBooks.
Plus, you'll be eligible for amazing contests, drawings, and
you'll receive immediate notice when my newest books become available!

Visit my website:
http://www.DonovanCreed.com

John Locke

New York Times Best Selling Author
8th Member of the Kindle Million Sales Club
*(which includes James Patterson, Stieg Larsson,
George R.R. Martin and Lee Child, among others)*

John Locke had 4 of the top 10 eBooks on
Amazon/Kindle at the same time, including #1 and #2!

...Had 6 of the top 20, and 8 books in the top 43
at the same time!

...Has written 19 books in three years in
four separate genres, all best-sellers!

...Has been published in numerous languages by many of the
world's most prestigious publishing houses!

Donovan Creed Series:
Lethal People
Lethal Experiment
Saving Rachel
Now & Then
Wish List
A Girl Like You
Vegas Moon
The Love You Crave
Maybe
Callie's Last Dance

Emmett Love Series:
Follow the Stone
Don't Poke the Bear
Emmett & Gentry
Goodbye, Enorma

Dani Ripper Series:
Call Me
Promise You Won't Tell?

Dr. Gideon Box Series:
Bad Doctor
Box

Other:
Kill Jill

Non-Fiction:
How I Sold 1 Million eBooks in 5 Months!

Made in the USA
Middletown, DE
19 November 2014